"You don't really know who I am or what I'm doing here," Jack said.

"You should be hysterical about now. Why aren't you?"

"Oh, please." Karina waved his question away. "I'm afraid hysteria is not my style."

His eyes narrowed thoughtfully. "You're taking this all too casually. Just for future reference, if a man ever comes bursting into your room again, I want you to scream this house down."

"Shall I do it now?" she asked obligingly.

"No!" Taking a quick step in her direction, he almost grabbed her, until he realized what he was doing, and stopped himself. "No, not now."

She gazed at him with ill-concealed amusement. "So you're the only man allowed to come in off my balcony. Is that it?"

He resisted the urge to grin at her, knowing very well it would be disaster to let her think he could treat her as a friend.

"You got it."

* * *

Jack and the Princess (SR April 2002)
Royal Nights (Sil. Single Title May 2002)
Betrothed to the Prince (SR June 2002)
Counterfeit Princess (SR July 2002)

ROMANCE

Dear Reader,

Spring cleaning wearing you out? Perk up with a heart-thumping romance from Silhouette Romance. This month, your favorite authors return to the line, and a new one makes her debut!

Take a much-deserved break with bestselling author Judy Christenberry's secret-baby story, *Daddy on the Doorstep* (#1654). Then plunge into Elizabeth August's latest, *The Rancher's Hand-Picked Bride* (#1656), about a celibate heroine forced to find her rugged neighbor a bride!

You won't want to miss the first in Raye Morgan's CATCHING THE CROWN miniseries about three royal siblings raised in America who must return to their kingdom and marry. In *Jack and the Princess* (#1655), Princess Karina falls for her bodyguard, but what will it take for this gruff commoner to win a place in the royal family? And in Diane Pershing's *The Wish* (#1657), the next SOULMATES installment, a pair of magic eyeglasses gives Gerri Conklin the chance to do over the most disastrous week of her life...and find the man of her dreams!

And be sure to keep your eye on these two Romance authors. Roxann Delaney delivers her third fabulous Silhouette Romance novel, *A Whole New Man* (#1658), about a live-for-the-moment hero transformed into a family man, but will it last? And Cheryl Kushner makes her debut with *He's Still the One* (#1659), a fresh, funny, heartwarming tale about a TV show host who returns to her hometown and the man she never stopped loving.

Happy reading!

Mary-Theresa Hussey

Mary-Theresa Hussey
Senior Editor

Please address questions and book requests to:
Silhouette Reader Service
U.S.: 3010 Walden Ave., P.O. Box 1325, Buffalo, NY 14269
Canadian: P.O. Box 609, Fort Erie, Ont. L2A 5X3

JACK
—AND THE—
PRINCESS

RAYE MORGAN

CATCHING
THE
CROWN

SILHOUETTE *Romance*®

Published by Silhouette Books

America's Publisher of Contemporary Romance

To royalty everywhere:
May they live on in our dreams
and stay out of our politics!

 SILHOUETTE BOOKS

ISBN 0-373-19655-5

JACK AND THE PRINCESS

Copyright © 2003 by Helen Conrad

This edition published by arrangement with Harlequin Books S.A.

® and TM are trademarks of Harlequin Books S.A., used under license.
Trademarks indicated with ® are registered in the United States Patent
and Trademark Office, the Canadian Trade Marks Office and in other
countries.

Visit Silhouette at www.eHarlequin.com

Printed in U.S.A.

Books by Raye Morgan

Silhouette Romance

Roses Never Fade #427
Promoted—To Wife! #1451
The Boss's Baby Mistake #1499
Working Overtime #1548
She's Having My Baby! #1571
A Little Moonlighting #1595
†*Jack and the Princess* #1655

Silhouette Books

Wanted: Mother
"The Baby Invasion"

Silhouette Desire

Embers of the Sun #52
Summer Wind #101
Crystal Blue Horizon #141
A Lucky Streak #393
Husband for Hire #434
Too Many Babies #543
Ladies' Man #562
In a Marrying Mood #623
Baby Aboard #673
Almost a Bride #717
The Bachelor #768
Caution: Charm at Work #807
Yesterday's Outlaw #836
The Daddy Due Date #843
Babies on the Doorstep #886
Sorry, the Bride Has Escaped #892
*Baby Dreams #997
*A Gift for Baby #1010
*Babies by the Busload #1022
*Instant Dad #1040
Wife by Contract #1100
The Hand-Picked Bride #1119
Secret Dad #1199

†Catching the Crown
*The Baby Shower

RAYE MORGAN

has spent almost two decades, while writing over fifty novels, searching for the answer to that elusive question: Just what is that special magic that happens when a man and a woman fall in love? Every time she thinks she has the answer, a new wrinkle pops up, necessitating another book! Meanwhile, after living in Holland, Guam, Japan and Washington, D.C., she currently makes her home in Southern California with her husband and two of her four boys.

THE NABOTAVIAN ROYAL FAMILY

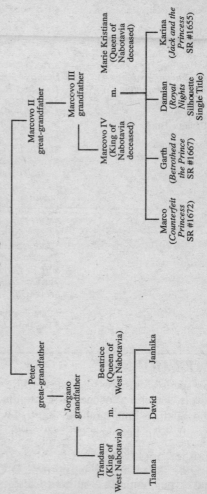

House of the White Rose
The Roseanova-Krimorovas
West Nabotavia

House of the Red Rose
The Roseanovas
Nabotavia

King Marcovo I
Royal House of the Rose
great-great grandfather

Peter
great-grandfather

Marcovo II
great-grandfather

Marcovo III
grandfather

Jorgano
grandfather

Marcovo IV
(King of
Nabotavia
deceased)

Marie Kristiana
(Queen of
Nabotavia
deceased)

Trandam
(King of
West Nabotavia)

m.

Beatrice
(Queen of
West Nabotavia)

m.

Tianna

David

Jannika

Marco
(*Counterfeit
Princess*
SR #1672)

Garth
(*Betrothed to
the Prince*
SR #1667)

Damian
(*Royal
Nights*
Silhouette
Single Title)

Karina
(*Jack and the
Princess*
SR #1655
deceased)

Chapter One

Scaling the wall of a mansion and slipping from a balcony into an upper-floor room was probably a unique way of interviewing for a job. But Jack Santini was a pretty unique guy, and he decided it was the reasonable way to go. And all went well until he got to his destination. He hadn't expected to find a young woman in the room, much less in the bed, in mid-afternoon. As he came in through the open French doors, he was as surprised as she was.

He couldn't afford to have her scream and bring the household down on top of him, so he followed his instincts and grabbed her quickly, covering her mouth with his hand while he whispered in her ear.

"Take it easy, honey. I'm not going to hurt you."

She didn't struggle. Her first start of alarm faded quickly, and though he could feel hear heart beating wildly, she was looking at him sideways, more with wide-eyed interest than with fear. She was a pretty one, with shiny golden hair that curled around her face and huge blue eyes framed by thick black lashes. For just a moment he was intensely aware of how soft and rounded she felt, and his head was filled with her fresh, sunshine scent. But he shook it off. Years of training held him in good stead and he quickly regained his professionalism.

"You think you can stay quiet for me?" he asked her, his mouth against her ear.

She nodded and he loosened his grip, waiting just a few seconds to make sure she wasn't bluffing before completely releasing her. Springing up off the bed, he went to the door and listened, ready to leave as quickly as he'd arrived. There were people in the hallway, chatting back and forth. Probably maids cleaning rooms. He combed a hand through his thick black hair, frustrated. He was going to have to get past them if he was going to end up downstairs in the business office without triggering any sort of alarm.

That was his goal. He'd come to interview for the job as head of security for this estate. He liked to take a direct approach and test out what was going on, which is why he'd come into the property the way he had. His experiment was showing him that security here needed a lot of work.

But his test wasn't over. He still had to arrive at estate manager Tim Blodnick's desk without being let in the front door. He was anticipating the look he would see on Tim's face when he appeared out of nowhere. The next few minutes after that look would determine whether he took the job or not. Even though he was desperate as hell for something to pull him out of the swamp he was stuck in, he wasn't about to sell his soul. Time would tell.

The best thing would be to show up in front of Tim's astonished face in about two minutes. But the voices still echoed up and down the hallway, sounding casual, in no hurry. He couldn't leave the room until they'd gone. Stymied, he glanced back at the girl on the bed.

She was sitting back against the headboard, watching him, her eyes very bright. She looked wary but not really scared, and he supposed that was a good thing, although rather unusual. One yell from her and he would seem foolish instead of exceptionally expert, which was what he was going for. He was lucky she was staying calm.

"Where are you taking me?" she asked him, acting more like someone on the brink of an adventure than anything else.

He turned fully and looked at her, noticing again that she was one of the prettiest girls he'd seen in a long time. An employee, probably. The room was sparse, with nothing more than a simple bed, a straight-backed chair and a small dresser. There were no decorations, no fancy drapes. The house itself had the look of a fairy-tale castle from the outside. If she was part of the family who lived here, he would think she would have fancier digs. At the most, he expected she might be a visiting granddaughter of the old couple Tim had mentioned lived in the place.

"I'm not taking you anywhere," he reassured her, starting back toward the door. "I'm getting out of here as soon as the coast is clear."

Her pretty face took on a puzzled frown. "Wait a minute. Didn't you come to kidnap me?"

He spun and stared at her, both hands raised. "Whoa, hold on. I'm not kidnapping anyone." He frowned, put off balance by her odd reactions. "Why would I want to kidnap you?"

Her chin lifted as though she was gathering pride around herself. "Because I'm the princess, of course."

A princess. Oh, sure. He relaxed. She certainly looked like one, though, sitting there in her lacy nightgown with her hair tumbling around her face. She could have been right out of a picture in a Victorian novel. Too bad she also seemed to be a little nuts. Either that, or she was just pulling his leg.

"A princess," he said wryly. "Right. And I'm Robin Hood."

Robin Hood. Karina Alexandera Roseanova, Princess of the Royal House of Nabotavia, mulled that over and it made her smile. This very imposing man would fit perfectly into the role of the bandit with a heart of gold. He moved with a strength and agility that made her marvel, and he had the right audacious attitude for it, as well.

She knew he was mocking her, but that didn't bother her at all. In fact, it made this encounter all the more interesting. She hardly ever got this close to such an attractive man—especially one who didn't know who she was. He was scoffing at the idea of her being a princess.

He didn't know!

This gave rise to all sorts of intriguing possibilities. She didn't get the chance to come across as a regular person very often. In fact, her life was often monotonous, although seldom ordinary. For her to sit here and contemplate being kidnapped and not be frightened by the prospect should have been bizarre, but somehow it wasn't. She knew very well that one of the main reasons they had to have such extensive security here at the estate was exactly because there *were* Nabotavian rebels who might think grabbing the princess would give them leverage of one sort or another.

There had been a coup in Nabotavia shortly after she was born. Her parents had been killed in the fighting, and she and her three brothers had been whisked out of the country for safekeeping. Ever since, fears that one of them might be grabbed and taken hostage in order to manipulate events back in the old country had been a constant backdrop to their lives. She knew she ought to take the risk more seriously, but she was tired of spending her life jumping at every strange sound and distrusting everyone who looked at her too long.

She'd lived that way for years; had endured being moved from one boarding school to another just when she'd finally made friends, because there might be a threat. She'd spent her summers in places so unpopular, no one under fifty could be seen on the streets;

and had sat through long dinners where her aunt and uncle and other relatives moaned and groaned about living in exile, while she dreamed of just being close enough to real life to see men who didn't wear dentures.

And now a gorgeous specimen of the most virile masculinity had been dropped right into her lap.

She watched as he went back to the door and pressed his ear to it, listening, it seemed, to see if the coast was clear. Remembering how it had felt when he'd held her in his arms, she shivered, even though she knew very well it had only been for emergency purposes. She hadn't had much male attention in her young life. That feeling was one she was going to cherish for a long time.

And she was going to need it, knowing the future she had in store for her. A shadow passed over her face as she thought of it, but she pushed it away quickly. She had the rest of the spring and most of the summer before her fate would be sealed. She meant to enjoy that small window of freedom to the hilt.

"You know..." she began, but he motioned for silence and she obeyed.

"Just a minute," he murmured, listening at the door and getting impatient. The maids were passing very close, laughing over some shared joke. If only they would get out of the hallway. At this rate he was going to be late, and the effect of his entrance wouldn't have nearly the same impact.

"Well," she began again, from right behind him this time.

He spun around, shocked that she had gotten up out of the bed and come so close without his noticing. He must be losing his edge. And guys in his business who lost their edge usually lost a lot more in the process. He was going to have to watch it.

"Shh," he warned her sternly.

She blinked and complied with his warning, going on in a stage whisper. "If you're not here to kidnap me, what are you here for?"

"Get back on the bed," he told her gruffly, feeling slightly dizzy from the sense of her warmth so close. He was tall and muscular, and suddenly he felt every bit of his manhood as he looked down at her delicate features. The white lace of her nightgown was edged by a threaded blue satin ribbon, emphasizing her femininity. She came to his shoulder, but her figure was slender. She looked light as a feather. Still, the outline of her breasts was clear through the lace, full and rounded and...

The bottom threatened to fall out of his stomach, like going fast over a dip in the road, and he had to look away quickly to keep control of his reactions. He'd just told her to do something, but he'd forgotten what it was, and she wasn't doing it, anyway. He frowned, trying to recapture his sense of reserve.

"You're not trying to burglarize us in broad daylight, are you?" she demanded as she thought of it. "Or maybe you're casing the joint?"

He had to look at her again at that one. She'd said

it oddly, and he suddenly realized she had a very slight accent. "'Casing the joint?'" he repeated, his tone shaded with just a little ridicule. "You've been watching too many old movies."

"And you're avoiding the question."

He supposed she deserved to know the truth. "Listen, you've got this all wrong. I'm not burglarizing anything. I'm just testing the security system on this estate, evaluating how tight it is."

She rolled her eyes. "'Just testing.' Right." She said it in a direct copy of the way he'd responded when she'd mentioned being a princess. "And I'm the chimney sweep."

He couldn't hold back the slow grin she evoked. She was darn cute, if annoying, with her tousled locks and her pert attitude. "Okay, chimney sweep," he said. "Because that really is what I'm doing. Just give me a minute and I'll be out of your hair."

The word triggered something between them. Her hand went involuntarily to smooth back her curls, and his gaze followed, caressing the golden cascade of hair for a moment, then sliding down to take in the way her breasts filled the bodice of her nightgown before he met her gaze and realized she'd noticed the way he was looking at her. Her huge blue eyes widened, and without saying another word, she reached out and took up a light robe that was slung across the back of a chair, slipping into it and pulling it together in front.

He felt his ears burn and wondered why. Suddenly, incredulously, he knew. Dammit, he was blushing.

That was what getting mixed up with women did for you. It was Eve with the apple every time—sweet temptation that you had to pay for, big-time, later on. With a soft, internal groan, he turned back to the door. There was still noise in the hallway. Without bad luck, he would have no luck at all.

"They'll be gone in a few minutes," she told him calmly. "They're a pair of chatterboxes."

"Maids?" he asked.

She nodded. "They would be in here right now, only they think I'm asleep. I'm just getting over the flu."

He glanced at her again, realizing that his attention was being drawn back to her repeatedly because she was just so good to look at. "I was wondering what you were doing in here at this time of the day."

She gazed at him levelly, her head to the side as she scanned him. "Since you figured out that I'm not the princess, what do you think I am?" Raising her arms, she turned before him, her eyes crinkling with amusement. "What do I look like to you?"

He would hate to say. She would probably slap his face if he were honest about it. "I don't know." He shrugged, put on a forced frown and went to the window, looking out at the rolling green lawn that was her view. You couldn't see the street from here, but he could see the tall wrought-iron fence that guarded the property. Everything else was trees. You would have thought this was out in the country somewhere. You couldn't really tell they were in the middle of

Beverly Hills. "Maybe a nanny for the little kids or something," he said back over his shoulder.

"You think I look like a nanny?" She seemed pleased as punch, turning to look in her mirror as if to confirm his opinion. And that just confused him all the more.

"You *do* work here, don't you?" he asked, just to make sure.

"Oh, yes." Turning back, she nodded wisely. "I work very hard, in fact."

"Do you? What do you do, exactly?"

"I…well…" She avoided his gaze, her attention skimming over the room. "You might say I'm a sort of companion to…to the princess." She gave him an impish grin. "There really is one, you know. And to the duchess."

"The duchess? What duchess?"

She turned to stare at him rather majestically. "Do you mean to tell me you broke into this house and you haven't any idea who lives here?"

"I haven't a clue."

"You see, that's your problem. If you did better research before you set up your breaking-and-entering projects, things might go more smoothly."

He knew she was trying to tease him, but he shrugged again. "It doesn't matter. My old friend Tim told me he had a job for me as head of security. I'm in real need of a job right now. He gave me the address and I came on over."

She drew in a quick breath. "So you're going to work here?"

"Maybe." He frowned at her, realizing she was going to be one of his charges if he did get the job. It was evident she needed a few lessons in how to protect herself. "You know what?" He jabbed a finger in her direction. "If I do, you're going to be one of my first cases. I'm worried about you."

"Me?" she squeaked, wide-eyed. "Why?"

He leaned toward her and she took a step back. "You don't really know who I am or what I'm doing here," he said accusingly. "You should be hysterical about now. Why aren't you?"

"Oh, please." She waved his question away. "I'm afraid hysteria is not my style."

His eyes narrowed thoughtfully. "You're taking this all too casually. Just for future reference, if a man ever comes bursting into your room again, I want you to scream this house down."

"Shall I do it now?" she asked obligingly.

"No!" Taking a quick step in her direction, he almost grabbed her, until he realized what he was doing and stopped himself. "No, not now."

She gazed at him with ill concealed amusement. "So you're the only man allowed to come in off my balcony. Is that it?"

He resisted the urge to grin at her, knowing very well it would be disaster to let her think he could treat her as a friend. "You got it. If I become head of security here, there are going to be some changes made."

"Well, I guess so." She was teasing him in earnest

now. "After all, old Mr. Sabrova never came into my room without knocking first."

"Who is old Mr. Sabrova?"

"The previous head of security. But then again, I don't think he could have made it up here even if he'd put a ladder up to the wall. He was pretty old. But a very nice man," she hastened to add, remembering her manners.

A very nice man, but like all the men around here, over-the-hill and not very interesting. After all, old Mr. Sabrova didn't have jet-black hair, thick as an animal pelt, and sexy muscles that bulged right through the fabric of his crisp white shirt and snug dark slacks, nor did he have stormy gray eyes that hinted at mysteries unlike anything she'd ever encountered.

"You're going to have to wear a uniform, you know," she told him, suppressing a grin as she thought of how he'd look in the ridiculous getup Mr. Sabrova had favored.

"I'm used to uniforms. I've been a Navy SEAL and a beat cop in my time." But then he remembered. This was a strange house with strange practices. He turned slowly and looked at her. "What sort of uniform?" he asked suspiciously.

"Oh, white with gold braid and epaulets on the shoulders and a red hat and—"

"No way." He laughed shortly. "That's not *my* style."

She gave him a skeptical look. "That's the way we do things here. That's the way it's always been."

"Tell you what. It may just be time to modernize this whole operation."

She laughed softly. "I can hardly wait to hear you tell that to the duchess."

He gazed at her quizzically. "Is there a 'mister duchess'?"

"Oh, yes. The duke. He's a darling. I adore him. But he doesn't matter. It's all her, believe me."

He held his hand up to stop her from saying anything while he listened intently.

"They're gone," he said decisively. He opened the door a crack and looked into the hallway. Glancing back, he winked at her. "Thanks for the memories," he said. "See you around." And he slipped out into the hallway, closing the door silently behind him.

Kari stared at the closed door for a moment, then moved resolutely toward the telephone on the corner of the dresser. Picking up the receiver, she pressed a few numbers and put it to her ear.

"Blodnick here," said the gruff male voice at the other end.

She smiled. "Mr. Blodnick, it's Kari. I believe you have an appointment today with a man—an old friend of yours—about taking on the job as head of security."

"You're right. He's late."

"No, on the contrary, he was here quite on time. I'm afraid I detained him."

"You what?"

The shock in his voice was palpable, but she ignored it.

"If at all possible, I'd like to have him hired, please."

There was a pause, and the man cleared his throat. Then he said the only thing he could say. "Whatever you say, Princess."

"Oh, and, Mr. Blodnick. About the uniform. I think you should discuss designing something new for the security guards. Your friend may have some ideas on that score. It is a new millennium, you know. We need to get with the times, don't you think?"

"Sounds doable, Princess."

"Thank you, Mr. Blodnick."

She hung up the telephone and smiled happily. Suddenly she didn't feel sick at all. Maybe this summer wasn't going to be quite the boring disaster she'd expected it to be. It was, after all, going to be her last period of relative freedom. And when it was over, she would be marrying someone her aunt chose for her. Something told her he wasn't going to be at all like the new head of security.

Her smile faded as she remembered that, and the familiar sensation of a fist closing down inside came over her. By winter she would be married and on her way back to Nabotavia, a place she didn't even remember.

"But that is weeks away," she told herself, closing her eyes and taking a deep, cleansing breath. "Weeks away."

Chapter Two

Jack tested the condition of the wrought-iron fence near where the hill rose behind the property and noted the results in his minirecorder. It was really too dark now to get a full picture, but he could see some of the more obvious features. He'd been head of security on this estate for all of six hours, and he'd already found a number of improvements that had to be made to bring the place up to standard, which was what he'd been told his goal would be, Upgrading conditions and managing a staff of five rotating guards were the main duties he'd signed on for. The pay was above average and included living quarters right here in the compound. It was a good job and he was glad he had it, if temporarily.

The estate was large, consisting of the main house, a few utility buildings, a five-car garage with chauffeur's quarters overhead, a garden house with the security office and the apartment where he would be staying. The grounds were extensive, including a small stand of redwoods that gave the sense of being in a forest, a formal rose garden that seemed to be a special showplace for the estate, emblematic to the royal family themselves, a kitchen garden and three small pools connected by waterfalls, ducks and koi. Another waterfall recycled water into the swimming pool. Everywhere there was the sound of water.

He still hadn't figured out exactly who this was he was working for. Tim had been in a hurry to make a meeting in L.A. and had promised to fill him in later. He gathered these people were some sort of exiled royalty from some little country in Europe—situated somewhere between Austria and Hungary—he'd never heard of before. They certainly employed a lot of people, most of them from the same little country. So far he'd seen three maids, a cook, a butler, two gardeners and a chauffeur, plus, of course, the "companion" whose room he'd invaded.

Thinking of her, he glanced up at the house, his gaze focusing immediately on the brightly lit window of the room where he'd been, and the memory of how soft and rounded she'd felt in his arms flashed in his mind. Resolutely he pushed the image away. She was dangerously attractive and deeply appealing, but he wasn't in the market for that sort of thing. Getting involved with a woman had messed him up one too many times. If he hadn't learned his lesson by now, there was no hope for him. He was going to have to keep his distance from that one. And that shouldn't be too hard to do. The security of the place needed a lot of work. He was going to be very busy.

And, turning to go back up toward the house, he nearly ran smack into the very woman he'd been trying to avoid thinking about.

"Whoa!" He jerked back, just missing her, and annoyed that he hadn't heard her approach. The ubiquitous waterfall sounds masked everything else. He was going to have to see about making some adjustments there.

"Hello," she said, glancing toward the house and stepping back farther into the shadows the long rose arbor made along the edge of the property. "I thought I might find you out here."

He frowned, not pleased to see her. She was too damn pretty for her own good. "I'm just going in," he said gruffly, and turned to go.

"Wait. I've brought you something."

He turned back and looked at what she was carrying, but he couldn't quite make out what it was in the darkness.

"I brought you a lemon tart from dinner. I know you didn't get one."

He hesitated, knowing he was being a fool. But a lemon tart—it was only his favorite food, and his stomach growled just to remind him that he was hungry as a bear. One little lemon tart. What could that hurt? Besides, it would be rude to cut her off when she was being so friendly. Reluctantly he turned back.

"Thanks," he said simply, and followed her back into the arbor to a bench where the light from the

lanterns around the nearby swimming pool brightened
the area. They both sat down, and she handed him
the plate and a fork.

He took a bite, savored it, then gave her a lopsided
grin. "Thanks a lot," he said sincerely. "This is really good."

She smiled back. She was glad she'd come out
now. At first she hadn't been sure. All through dinner
she'd watched for him out of the tall dining room
windows, but she hadn't caught sight of him. So she'd
decided to take a chance once her aunt was safely off
to visit her friend who lived a few blocks away. She'd
gone to the kitchen, snatched a lemon tart and come
out searching. Luckily she'd found him right away.

"So, Mr. Jack Santini," she said, showing off that
she'd found out what his name was. "You decided to
take the job."

"A man's got to eat," he said, taking another bite
of the tart as though to illustrate that very concept.
"And from what I've seen so far, you people eat
pretty well."

She supposed that was true. They employed a wonderful cook. The food here at her aunt's was certainly
better than anything she'd ever been given at any of
the many boarding schools she had attended. One of
her goals for the summer was to learn to cook. What
if it was true that good food was the way to a man's
heart? Hmm...

She looked at him and felt a ripple of excitement
flow through her. He was so attractive, so...well, so
male. What could she do to get him to stay with her

a little longer after he'd finished the dessert? Maybe she could get him to talk.

"Tell me about yourself," she said brightly. "Are you married?"

He took a last bite of the tart and gazed at her levelly. She was dressed in a sweater and slacks and had her hair tied back in a ponytail that looked completely appropriate. She seemed impossibly young. And young was something he had never seemed to be.

He wasn't sure if he'd always been such a pessimist, but lately it felt as though his life always had a sense of waiting for the ax to fall, wondering when things would get worse. And they usually did. Right now he was on suspension from the police department, cut off from the career as a police detective that he loved, taking this job to fill in the gap and hold him over until a hearing on his future was held.

It wasn't as if he was complaining. The suspension was his own fault. He knew very well what he'd done. Given the same circumstances, he very likely would do the same thing over again. His instincts always seemed to put him in position to go overboard protecting someone else—particularly if she was a woman—and end up hurting himself. He had to be careful not let that happen anymore.

And he had to be careful not to let anything he did here make things worse as far as his suspension went. And how could that happen? Well, he could let himself get involved in a flirtation with this pretty young thing. That ought to just about seal the deal on his doom. But he wasn't quite that stupid. Or that weak.

And she wanted to know if he was married. He gave her a sideways look and said, "Why would you care about a thing like that?"

"No reason. I'm just making small talk."

"Small talk." He couldn't help it. She made him want to laugh. "Okay, here's some fodder for your small talk. I'm thirty years old. I was born in San Diego, grew up all over the place. Was a Navy SEAL for a few years, then joined the Rancho Diego Police Department. I was engaged once, for about five minutes. But I've never been married. And I have no kids."

He left out a few things, such as the fact that his parents had died in a car accident when he was young and he'd been shuttled from one place to another, living with various relatives, until finally he'd ended up in a group home for problem teenagers. He understood that his early rootless existence was behind his strong need to find his identity in organizations such as the police force. But that understanding didn't make the need any less powerful.

"Whew." She whipped her head around as though she'd just been hit with a strong wind. "I guess that takes care of that. Now I feel like I've known you all my life."

He handed her his empty plate, knowing it was time to get up and walk away. But that would be a little abrupt. He supposed he could spare a few minutes to be courteous. "You may know me, but I don't know you," he told her. "Your turn."

She blanched and looked away, using the moment to set the plate down on the bench beside her. She'd almost forgotten that he didn't know yet who she was. He would know soon enough—perhaps in minutes. But she wanted to prolong him not knowing as long as she could. She hated the way people changed once they were told she was royal.

Sometimes she wished she could shed that royalty like a used and useless second skin, cast it off like a worn-out dress. She'd been quite rebellious about it a few years ago as a teenager.

After all, to her, royalty meant such loneliness. Since the loss of her parents, when she was a baby, she'd always had her aunt and uncle. But her brothers had been raised elsewhere. The two oldest, Crown Prince Marco and Prince Garth, had been raised by another uncle at his family home in Arizona. Prince Damian, the closest to her in age, spent most of his early years living with their mother's twin sister and her family. She had only seen them all on special occasions. For most of her youngest years, she'd lived under the rule of a governess. Children were occasionally carted in to play with her, but the situation was hit-and-miss. She was excited when she went away to school at fourteen. Finally she would meet people of her own age.

But developing relationships was still hard as she moved to each school with a whole retinue, taking over entire sections of the dormitory like an occupying force. That, combined with the fact that she changed schools so often, meant that friendships were still tough.

She hoped things would be different once she was married. Though she hardly expected to find true love in an arranged marriage, she did expect her mate would be a friend, someone to talk to, someone to share life with. She'd settled down now. Her small flash of rebellion was in the past. She was sworn to do her duty and she was ready to fulfill her role. She only hoped she would marry a man she could like.

That was the current state of her affairs, of who she was, but Jack Santini didn't want to hear all of that.

"I'm not very interesting," she said quickly. "I'll tell you something about the family, though. What would you like to know?"

"Your name, for starters."

Her name. Well, that was easy. "Kari."

"Kari." He said it slowly, as though he wanted to remember it, and that made her smile. "Just Kari?" he added.

"Isn't that enough?"

"Most people have a last name, too."

She shook her head. "I've got too many of them. They would only confuse you." She turned to look at the swimming pool through the leaves of the rose vines. The light from the lanterns made ghostly reflections on the inky water. "But we were talking about the family. Aren't you curious about them?"

"The family." He considered for a moment. "Okay. Tell me what I should know."

"The Roseanovas are a very old family. They ruled Nabotavia for almost a thousand years. Then, twenty years ago they were overthrown by rebels. The December Radicals, they were called." She rolled her eyes to show what she thought of them. "The king and queen were killed...."

She stopped, surprised that her voice was quavering over that last statement. It was her own parents she was talking about. It had been so long ago, when she was just a baby, and she didn't remember them, except for what she knew from old pictures and stories. She'd thought she was used to that, but for some reason, her voice was betraying emotions she thought she'd tamed. Taking a deep breath, she went on. "And many others were forced to flee from the country."

"Including you."

"Oh, yes. Also the duke and the duchess, and—"

"And the princess? I've been told there really is a princess."

She nodded, eyes sparkling. "And you doubted me," she charged. "The princess was smuggled out of the country, along with her three older brothers." Then she looked at him curiously. "What did they tell you about her?"

He shrugged and stretched back, leaning against the railing with his legs extended out before him. "Nothing. Tim was more concerned that I not get on the wrong side of the duchess than anything else." He cocked an eyebrow. "Is that the duchess you were talking about?"

She nodded. "Yes."

"So she's pretty hard to please, is she?"

Kari hesitated. She didn't want to say anything against her aunt. After all, the woman had raised her—in a way. How could she put this delicately? "You know the wicked stepmother in the Cinderella story?" she ventured.

He grinned, his white teeth flashing in the gloom. "Sure."

She gave a soft laugh. "She's sort of like an updated version of her."

He chuckled. "And what are you? Cinderella? Do they make you do all the dirty chores?"

"Not quite. But there are certain expectations and standards that must be met." She waved the topic away. "But you'll see for yourself tomorrow. She's planning to have Mr. Blodnick perform an introduction. Something of a royal audience," she added with a gleam in her eye that was close to teasing.

He noticed. She was getting more and more familiar with him. He knew he ought to get up off the bench and head for somewhere as far as possible away from this beguiling female. But for some reason he just couldn't do it. Instead he turned away again and sat staring off toward the swimming pool, telling himself not looking at her would be almost as good as leaving. And knowing he was lying.

"So I'm going to meet the people I'm working for," he noted with a shrug. "That's pretty routine, don't you think?"

"Oh, not at all. It's very important that the duchess and the princess approve of you."

"I've got no reason to think they won't," he said with complete confidence. "I know what I'm doing. And I'm a likable guy, after all."

She studied him critically, her head to the side. Likable was one thing. Absolutely gorgeous was another. What would her aunt think of having her guarded by a man like this? Wouldn't she have second thoughts? Wouldn't she notice that an electricity seemed to spark between them at times? And once she did notice, wouldn't she get rid of this man as quickly as possible?

The answer to most of those questions of course was yes. It was going to be up to Kari to find a way to make sure she didn't think them.

"Well, the duchess won't like you, no matter how nice you are, because the duchess doesn't like anyone," she told him pertly, overstating the case, but only a little. "But the princess…now that's another matter." She pretended to think hard, her brow furled. "What will the princess think of you?"

He had to turn and look at her. There was something odd about her tone of voice, and he couldn't quite put his finger on what it was. He knew she was teasing again, but he wasn't sure why.

"What's she like?" he asked, watching her face.

"The princess?" She shuddered. "Oh, she's ugly as a bulldog. She's slow and dull and she has no real wit about her."

He stared at her for a moment, then a reluctant

smile quirked the corners of his wide mouth. "You're a real good friend of hers, are you?"

"Oh, very," she said in all sincerity. "We're close as...as...as sisters."

"Sisters." He nodded, and his smile took on a more cynical twist. "Funny, I heard she was pretty." He watched for her reaction.

And she gave him one, rolling her eyes. "You know how people are sometimes. They endow celebrities with beauty and talent they don't really have, just because they *are* celebrities. Well, people do the same thing with royalty."

"Do they?"

"Oh, yes. I've seen men look at the princess and not even notice that she squints and walks into walls and that her feet stick out at funny angles." She nodded emphatically, her eyes shimmering with laughter. "I've even heard people say she's beautiful." She shrugged, hands out in a "go figure" gesture.

"Poor, demented souls." He was laughing at her now.

"Exactly!" She laughed back. "That's how blind people can be."

Their gazes connected and suddenly she was aware of how soft the air felt, how different from anything she'd ever noticed before. She sobered, still looking into his eyes and feeling very strange, almost like floating.

"Are you saying I'm blind, too?" he asked, though his voice seemed to have dropped an octave.

"Oh, no," she assured him. "I just wanted to warn

you, so you could be prepared.'' She caught the hint of a clean, masculine scent and wondered if it were a flower blooming nearby or his aftershave. She wanted to get closer, just to see. ''I wouldn't want you to fall into that trap,'' she added somewhat breathlessly.

''Why?'' he asked her lazily, his eyes half-closed. ''Are you afraid I'm going to fall for the princess?''

Her shrug had a sensual languor to it that made him think—for some reason—of naked bodies on satin sheets.

''You might,'' she murmured, her gaze locked with his. ''Stranger things have happened.''

The magnetic pull between them seemed to have a life of its own, generating heat and electricity that made Jack feel it was inevitable that they would kiss. The soft darkness, the sound of water, the scent of roses, all combined to draw them closer and closer. But Jack had the sense and experience to know what was happening, and he knew it was wrong—and that he was the one who had to stop it. He started to straighten, to pull away, but Kari stopped him.

''Hold still,'' she said. ''You've got a smudge on your face.''

It was only a crumb from the pie crust on the lemon tart, caught by the barely visible beginnings of a growth of dark beard alongside his mouth. Her heart began to pound as she leaned forward to get it. What was she doing? She had no idea, but she wanted to touch him so badly. Reaching out, she brushed the crumb away, then let her fingers linger there as she looked up into his eyes, just inches away from hers. A change came over them as she watched. She saw a darkening, as though a cloud had covered the sun, and then she caught her breath. For the first time in her life, she saw raw desire in a man's eyes and knew it was aimed at her.

The strange thing was, it didn't frighten her at all. Instead, a thrill shivered through her, making her feel alive as she'd never felt before. Her hand turned, cupping his cheek with her palm and fingers, and she looked at his lips, suddenly needing his kiss as though it would keep her from dying. Her own lips parted and she drew closer...closer...her heart beating wildly, her blood singing in her veins.

Jack's groan came from deep within his soul and it came with an effort he was almost too overcome to make. Reaching up, he circled her wrist with his fingers and pushed her hand away.

"You'd better go in," he said roughly, hoping she didn't notice that his breath was coming too quickly, that his own heart was beating right along with hers. He didn't think he'd ever felt this aroused before without doing something about it. Why it had happened so quickly and so effortlessly with this woman he barely knew, he wasn't sure. He only knew he had to avoid the temptation she represented if he wanted to keep from ruining his own future—and that he had to protect her from himself.

That she was an innocent was obvious. That her naiveté seemed to excite him in a way he hadn't been excited in a long, long time was not something he was particularly proud of. His first instincts had been right on the money. He was going to have to avoid her at all costs.

Suddenly they were both aware of voices. They turned and looked toward the house. A figure filled the lit window of Kari's room.

"Oh-oh!" Kari jumped up from the bench, picking up the plate as she went. "I'm going to have to go in. The duchess is looking for me." She flashed him a quick, wavering smile. "Good night."

He watched her go and groaned again, leaning his head back against the railing. Five minutes with the woman and he was thinking about how she would fit into his bed. And she was the kind of woman that had "trouble" written all over her. If he was going to give in to the urge to mess around, it would have to be with a woman who had been there and done that and knew the score, not some sweet little innocent looking for someone to love. How had he let that happen? Whatever it had been—it couldn't happen again. If he had to get tough, that was exactly what he would have to do. But he had to stay away from Kari. That much was a given.

He was a little out of his depth here. What was he—an ordinary police detective, a guy who'd grown up in foster homes with no family of his own, who'd had to struggle to get an education and build a life for himself, with no background to depend on—doing here, working for royalty? Oh, well, it was just for the summer, just until he could get reinstated for his job. He supposed he ought to appreciate the experience. He would never have another one quite like it.

Chapter Three

"Karina, will you stop looking at yourself in the mirror?"

The duchess glared adamantly across her impressively decorated dressing room at her charge. They were prepared to go out to an engagement, but were waiting for Tim Blodnick to announce that he was downstairs and ready to introduce them to Jack Santini.

"You're developing an unhealthy interest in your own reflection."

Kari took one last look at the impeccably dressed woman in the mirror and sighed. For the first time in her life she actually cared how she looked in more than a passing way. She would have thought her aunt would be glad she was finally taking something of an interest.

The image was of a slim young woman wearing a

royal-blue silk sheath with princess seams and a scooped neckline. She had on white gloves and spectator pumps. A small pillbox hat with a skimpy veil for decoration sat perched atop hair that was carefully arranged in a comely twist. And, of course, she sported tasteful pearls. No princess of her age would go out without them. At least, that was what her aunt always told her.

She looked like a picture from a history book. What would happen if she ripped off these relics and put on a nice tight sweater and a leather skirt? Her aunt would have her committed, no doubt about it.

"First you tell me to take a look at myself more often and try to make my image conform to what a princess should look like," she commented. "Then you criticize me for doing exactly that."

The duchess turned and gave her an assessing look. The woman herself looked well groomed and elegant in an obviously expensive lime-green silk suit that suited her coloring. Her hair was cut short and chic and dyed an attractive shade of silver. She looked altogether imposing, which was precisely what she was.

"It is very important to get the look exactly right," she counseled her niece. "But it is just as important not to let anyone know it was any effort. Your royal style should flow naturally, like the waters of the Tannabee River that runs through the heart of Nabotavia." She made an elegant gesture with her hand. "Perfection is fundamental and imperative. But never allow anyone to see you attempting to achieve it."

Kari smiled to cover the annoyance she felt. She wanted to let it out, to rip the hat off and toss it out the window, to trade in her dress for jeans and a tummy-tickler T-shirt. She wanted to be a normal and very casual young woman, just like the young women she saw from the limousine window as she was whisked from one official engagement to another.

Well, she couldn't do that. But sometimes her sharp tongue was just too quick to be stopped. "I see," she said brightly. "In other words, all's fair in the quest for royal superiority. Lie, cheat and steal—just don't get caught."

The duchess turned away, looking in need of smelling salts. "Much too vulgar for a princess," she murmured faintly, but, glancing at her diamond-studded watch, she quickly regained her sharply efficient attitude.

"I hope Mr. Blodnick hurries along and brings this new fellow he's hired as head of security. I'm not sure I approve of this move he's made. I usually expect to meet the management-level employees before they are offered a contract."

Kari turned away and hummed a little tune trying to look innocent. If she told her aunt that she'd been behind the quick approval of the man, she knew very well her aunt would fire him on the spot. The duchess would be great at marshaling armies and taking over small countries, but she didn't have a lot of understanding in her soul.

She would certainly never understand what had happened in the arbor last night. But then, Kari didn't really understand it either. All she knew was that all she had to do was think about almost kissing Jack Santini and her breath stopped in her throat. She had been so forward! She knew very well that it had been her doing the seducing, not him. In fact, she didn't like to think about how he had reacted, because it made her worry that he'd been laughing at her the whole time. Had he thought she was silly?

No. Whenever she remembered the way he had groaned, as though he'd had to rip the sound out of somewhere deep and tortured, she got chills. She didn't think he'd been laughing. But still, she didn't know what he thought and that was making her nervous.

"Karina, please, don't slouch like a teenager."

She straightened without really hearing what the woman was saying. That was actually her usual reaction to the constant stream of advice and reproach. She usually got along well enough with her aunt, but it was her uncle she loved. The duke was her father's half brother, and to her, an orphan left alone in a very scary world, he represented parental love in a way her aunt never could. Her aunt was the taskmaster, the instructor, the maker of hated rules and regulations, Her uncle was the man who had taught her how to whistle, how to find the Big Dipper on a clear night, how to tell robins from blue jays. He was the one who read bedtime stories to a sleepy little girl, who always had her favorite candy hidden in his coat pocket, who carried her up to bed when she fell asleep over her toys. And though he had retreated more and more from any sphere where his wife took charge, he was always available for Kari when she needed someone to talk to.

The telephone rang and the duchess took it. "He's ready," she told Kari. "Let's go down."

Kari hesitated, her pulse speeding up just a bit. She had to admit she was just a little nervous. She was looking forward to seeing Jack again, and yet she wasn't looking forward to his reaction once he realized she was the princess. She didn't think he'd guessed—although someone might have told him by now. Maybe when she walked into the room he would already know and she wouldn't have to see the look of shock in his eyes as he realized what she'd kept from him.

As she followed her aunt down the stairs, she realized she was dreading that. At first she'd thought it would be fun—that he would look surprised and she would laugh. But having gotten to know him a little better last night, she knew that wasn't what was going to happen. He wasn't going to like the fact that she'd tricked him.

"Duchess Irinia Roseanova, allow me to introduce Jack Santini, our new manager of estate security."

She came into the room just in time to see Tim present Jack to the duchess, but not in time to be addressed along with her. Jack's attention was all on her aunt and that was just as well. She hung back, waiting for him to look around and notice her.

"We've lived very quietly recently, Mr. Santini," the duchess was saying. "But all that is going to change as spring opens into summer. We have a number of entertainments planned, and we will need extra security during them.''

''What sort of entertainments do you have in mind?'' he asked.

''We will be giving dinners, card parties, a tea or two and, of course, the ball.''

''A ball?''

''Yes. The ball will be held at the country club, not here on our premises. However, I'll expect you to be in charge of security for the ball, and that will entail quite a bit of work. We're expecting almost two hundred people to attend.''

They went on talking about plans, and Kari watched on tenterhooks. Jack was dressed in black slacks, a black long-sleeved shirt and a silver tie. She wondered if this would be the new uniform, and that made her smile. He was so very handsome. Still waiting, she tugged off her gloves and held them in one hand. When he was presented and he bent to kiss her fingers, she wanted his lips to touch flesh, not fabric.

And suddenly he was coming her way and looking right at her, and Tim was saying, ''And I believe you've met the princess casually, but I'd now like to make a formal introduction. Princess Karina Alexandera Roseanova, may I present Jack Santini?''

Tim turned back to speak to the duchess, leaving Kari and Jack to deal with the rest of the introduction alone. She raised her gaze to meet Jack's and found it unreadable. That only made her more uneasy, so she held her head high and extended her left hand in a formal, if rather haughty, manner.

He took it gingerly, looked down at it, then back into her eyes. "What am I supposed to do with this limp fish?" he asked in a low voice just loud enough for her to hear.

She caught her breath. He was angry. Well, she supposed she couldn't blame him. But neither could she let on to her aunt that there was any sort of relationship between them.

"It is customary that you kiss my hand," she told him imperiously, keeping her gaze cool and distant.

Grabbing her hand more firmly, he used it to pull her closer and murmured, "I'd rather spank your bottom," before he let her go.

"Oh!"

Her cheeks colored and her blue eyes glittered and he immediately regretted what he'd done. But not very much. He was quite serious. The girl needed a little discipline. He felt like a fool and he was furious with her for leading him on and letting him say stupid things. Still, there was a facade here that had to be maintained.

He brushed her fingers with his lips and then dropped her hand like a hot potato.

"So happy to meet you, Princess," he said, sarcasm spicing his tone.

But then his gaze met hers again and he saw her remorse. His anger began to fade. After all, what had it really hurt for him to think she was just an employee for a time? Thank God he hadn't taken advantage of the kiss she'd offered him the night before. At least there was that.

"I'm glad to see that your squint has healed, Princess," he added, just to show her he was still annoyed, but wasn't going to hold it against her. "And that you are no longer walking into walls."

She bit back a smile, obviously relieved but still looking a bit contrite. "Yes, I'm doing very well," she said coolly, her nose in the air. "With therapy, I may even get my feet to go straight again."

The duchess turned from her talk with Tim and frowned in their direction. "Karina. Is something wrong?"

Kari sent a brilliant smile in her direction. "Oh, no, madam. Nothing at all."

They waited for the duchess to resume her talk with Tim, and then Jack leaned closer and said, "You could have told me the truth."

Her eyes flashed as she looked at him. "I did. You were the one who refused to believe it."

He knew she was right but he hated to admit it. Of course, if he'd only thought about it, he would have known. The clues were everywhere for him to see. As he thought back over their conversation the night before, he could see that she'd practically spelled it out for him. He was the one who'd been too dense to put two and two together. Well, what did it matter, anyway? Her being the princess only made it more imperative that he stay away from her. Maybe it was all to the good.

She turned to walk toward the windows, pulling her

gloves on as she went, and he followed her, no longer annoyed with her and rather captivated by the quaint picture she made, all decked out in her old-fashioned attire.

"You look like something out of the fifties," he told her softly as they stopped to gaze out over the lawn. "What's the deal with the little hat?"

She touched it and smiled. "That's the way we royalty are supposed to be, you know," she told him. "Timeless. Classic. Straight out of the past and walking boldly into the future."

She looked up at him, laughter in her eyes, and he found himself smiling down at her.

A princess. What the hell had he gotten himself into here?

But their moment was already over. Tim and the duchess were coming toward where they stood at the window, and the duchess was addressing him. He turned to face her.

"I'm glad to have met you, Mr. Santini," she was saying, looking very regal. "I'm sure you will do a splendid job, as long as you stick to the basics. Right now we're going to need someone to accompany us for the afternoon. We are going to a Ladies' League meeting. Princess Karina will be the guest of honor at their tea, where she will present a short speech on the history of Nabotavia and the latest developments from that part of the world. Even in such a benign setting, she must be guarded, you know."

"Very well, madam," Jack said mildly. He'd already known about this and was prepared. His gaze skimmed over Kari's and away again. "I've assigned Will Strator to accompany you. He should be waiting in the driveway at this very moment."

He didn't have to look at Kari to sense her disappointment. She'd thought he might be coming along. Well, he wasn't going to get caught in that game. He had other guards who could watch Kari when she went out in public. He wasn't going to do it.

"Goodbye," she murmured as she slipped past him. "You're missing a great speech."

She left her scent behind, and he inhaled it for a moment before turning away to get back to work. And then he wished he hadn't. Memorizing the perfume she wore would only make it worse when he thought of her at night. Because that was all he was going to do. No doubt about it. This was more of a hands-off situation than ever. The woman was a princess for God's sake. As if things weren't bad enough.

Three Days Later

"Oh, Mr. Santini."

Jack turned back. The duchess had just finished filling him in on some changes she wanted made to the alarm system and was calling him back as an afterthought.

"The princess has an appointment to make some dress selections at Goldmar's at two o'clock. She'll be going alone, as I have some visitors coming. But she'll need protection."

Jack gritted his teeth. Every man he had available

was already assigned. "I'm afraid we don't have anyone free at this time," he started to tell the duchess.

"Then you'll have to go with her," she said impatiently. "Protecting the princess is your first priority. Never forget that."

Of course it was, and he felt it as strongly as anyone. He knew she couldn't go out alone. He'd been briefed about the Nabotavian rebels and the threats that were periodically made against the family, and against Kari in particular. It was a turbulent time for the country, with the rebels losing favor with the population and a constitutional monarchy being restored. From what he gathered, there were numerous factions from the old country who would like nothing better than to get their hands on the popular princess in order to push their own agenda. Of course keeping her safe was the most important part of his job. He'd hoped the appointment might be canceled, but it didn't seem to be an option.

"Of course I'll handle it," he told her crisply. "I'll be ready at one-thirty."

In the three days since the introduction in the parlor, he'd managed to find ways to stay out of Kari's path for all that time. He was getting pretty good at knowing instinctively when she was liable to show up in any given area, and in making himself scarce at just the right moment. He'd even managed to stop thinking about her forty times an hour as he had at first. He was on the right track. As long as he kept his distance, the temptation she represented would fade more and more.

The worst had been the day it had been warmer than usual and a group of Nabotavians who lived in another part of the state had arrived for a visit. The party had included two young women about Kari's age, and the three of them had gone for a swim. Though he'd heard the laughter and the splashing, he hadn't thought much about it. But when he walked out of the guard office, there Kari had been, poised on the diving board, about to take a plunge into the water, wearing an alluring one-piece suit. She'd been calling to one of the others and hadn't noticed him, and that was lucky, because he'd turned to stone for a moment, unable to move, as he'd stared at her, every masculine response in his body coming alive and aching.

She'd been so beautiful in an innocent, untouched way. Her skin had gleamed golden in the sunlight, her hair a golden-blond halo around her pretty face. Her slim body was perfect, with her breasts swelling inside the swimsuit top; her long, graceful legs and those intoxicating curves. Desire had risen in him like smoke from a fire, and he'd choked on it.

He'd finally gotten himself under control and turned away, muttering every obscenity he could think of under his breath as he got out of there as quickly as he could. But the picture of her poised in the air like a bird would stay with him for the rest of his life, no matter how hard he tried to erase it.

So he approached their impending outing with some reluctance, but when he met Kari at the car, she gave him a brief smile and entered the large Cadillac, inviting him to sit in the back with her. He sank into the luxurious seating, trying to forget what he knew about the body beside him so modestly clothed in a chic linen pants suit. After only a quick glance her way, he sat looking straight ahead as the chauffeur began to guide the car out onto the city streets. They rode along in silence for some time, and he'd just about decided that she'd taken the hint to heart and realized that they shouldn't attempt to have any sort of relationship when she spoke.

"Why do you hate me?" she asked softly.

He looked at her, startled. She was staring straight ahead. He glanced at Mr. Barbera, the chauffeur. There was a Plexiglas barrier between the front and back seats, but he knew that didn't always mean that sound wasn't traveling from one side to the other.

"Don't worry, he can't hear us," she said, still staring ahead and letting her lips move only slightly as she spoke. "He's half-deaf. But he can see. And he will tell everything he sees to my aunt, you can count on it."

How reassuring. Jack sighed, wishing he were anywhere but here.

"I don't hate you," he said, following her example of moving his lips only as much as he absolutely had to and staring out the window while he spoke.

"You've been avoiding me like the plague."

"I'm not avoiding you," he lied. "I'm just trying to do my job."

"I thought we could be friends."

There was no particular overt emotion in her voice,

but he thought he heard something—some tiny tremor, some vague vibration—that made him look at her again.

"Kari...Princess." He turned his head away again. "Look. You're royalty. I'm the serf, or whatever. I work for you. We are on completely different levels. It's hard to be friends that way."

Her outrage at that statement made her careless, and she completely forgot to hide what she had to say, turning to him and demanding, "What! Did you grow up in Europe or something? You sound more like a Nabotavian than I do. We're in the U.S.A. Everyone is supposed to be equal."

He frowned, talking directly to her. "There are always levels, even if people pretend to ignore them. Be realistic."

They had arrived at the large exclusive department store and Mr. Barbera was pulling up before the entrance. A doorman rushed to get the car door. Without saying anything more, Jack got out and helped Kari to her feet. Giving the chauffeur a wave, she turned toward the store and he went with her.

"Anyway," she said in a conversational voice as they walked along through the fine jewelry depart ment. "I'm not asking you to marry me. I just want you to be my friend."

They came to an elevator and stood side by side, waiting for the doors to open.

"You know you want more than a friend," he told her softly, watching to make sure they were not being overheard by any of the customers. After all, he shouldn't be talking this way to her. But he didn't have much choice.

"How do you know what I want?" she demanded, turning to look up at him, her blue eyes huge.

He hesitated. This really wasn't the time or the place. But once begun, this topic was pretty difficult to abandon until it had been dealt with. He looked down into her eyes and felt something twist in his chest. If only she weren't so damn appealing.

"The vibes between us tell it all," he told her shortly, willing her to understand without too much explanation.

"Vibes!" She said the word as though she scorned it.

The elevator doors opened and they went aboard. Jack pushed the button to close the door quickly so that they wouldn't have to share the elevator with anyone else. He had a feeling she would continue this conversation no matter who was listening.

Once they were underway, he turned to her. "Yes, vibes. You feel it, I feel it. If we hang around together too much, something is bound to happen."

Her eyes were even larger now, and they seemed to melt as he looked into them.

"Will it?" she said softly.

"Yes." Every part of him wanted to take her in his arms. Something about her looked so vulnerable right now. He wanted to reassure her, tell her not to worry. But he hardened his heart. "I've got more experience at this type of thing than you do. I know it will."

The doors opened on their floor. They stepped out. The showroom was before them, and a beautifully groomed woman was smiling in their direction. Kari looked around, then turned and grabbed his hand.

"Let's not argue anymore," she said, giving him a wobbly smile. "Let's just enjoy the afternoon."

He blinked. Didn't she get it? He was working here. He pulled away from her.

"I'll stay in the background and stand against the wall while you…"

"Oh, no you don't. You'll come on in with me." Her smile brightened as she took his arm. "They don't know I'm a princess. To these people, I'm just another spoiled girl from Beverly Hills. It would be perfectly natural for me to have my boyfriend along." Perfectly natural and perfectly normal. Things she would love to be. Things she really couldn't have. But just this once…

He was shaking his head, though he knew it wasn't going to make any difference. "Princess, I don't think this is a good idea."

"Please. I want you to."

He stared down into her beautiful eyes and swallowed hard. He should say no, He tried. But he couldn't do it.

"All right," he heard himself say.

She beamed up at him. "Good!" And she led him into the showroom.

Chapter Four

The showroom attendants were prepared for Kari and quickly accommodated her guest. A table had been set up in front of the stage. She and Jack sat down next to each other.

"We have a nice viewing ready for you, Miss Roseanova," the coolly efficient looking young woman told her. "Your aunt asked that you be shown a selection from a number of lines. If you would prefer to limit the number—"

"Oh, no. I want to see it all. Oh, and we'd like tea, please. And scones would be nice, don't you think?" Kari smiled at Jack, then at the helpful attendant. "Thank you very much."

Jack leaned close and muttered, "What are you doing?"

"I already know what dress I'm ordering," she told

him softly. "But the more I look at, the more time we'll have to talk."

"Talking isn't part of my job," he reminded her grimly, his gray gaze flickering in her direction and then away again.

"Maybe not, but keeping me happy is."

His face darkened, and she knew right away she'd said exactly the wrong thing. Catching her lower lip with her teeth, she winced, staring straight ahead. That had sounded bratty and immature and she deeply regretted it. Right then and there she vowed she would never let herself sound like that again. She tried to think of a way to take her words back, but it was too late as the first of the models began to mince across the stage.

The model paused, posing, but her gaze flickered over Jack before she got it under control. Kari stifled a chuckle. She nodded to the model and then to the attendant, who wrote down her wishes on the order slip. Kari took the opportunity to lean close to Jack and whisper to him.

"Do women always look at you like that?"

He raised an eyebrow innocently, "Like what?"

Her eyes sparkled. "You know very well what she was doing."

But another model had taken the stage, and it was time to examine the heavy silk gown she was displaying. One after another they came, while a background tape playing gentle standards filled in the atmosphere, but Kari hardly noticed. A few she ordered set aside, most she didn't, but her mind was much more on her companion than it was on the dresses.

He was sitting very still, and yet she thought she could feel that he was very alert, his senses on guard, his mind weighing everything. She had the urge to distract him, to make him pay more attention to Kari, the woman, rather than the princess who needed to be guarded. But she curbed her impulse. She wanted his respect as much as she wanted anything, and if that meant she would have to apply a little dignity to her bearing, that was what she would do.

Finally the attendant announced an intermission and the scones and tea were served on lovely porcelain china with sterling silver utensils. Kari took a sip of the hot liquid and smiled at the man by her side.

"You're bored to tears," she said calmly. "But you're very good at hiding it."

"I could never be bored around you, Princess," he said softly.

And it was true enough on a human level. Though he had some reservations about spending all this time merely sitting in a department store showroom, gazing at models and indulging a pretty princess, it did seem to be part of the job. This was a far cry from his usual routine, where periods of investigation and analysis were interspersed with violent episodes— short and dangerous but ultimately rewarding when criminals got the prosecution they deserved.

The rewards here were very different, he admitted to himself as he gazed at Kari's pretty face. Different...but just as dangerous.

"I'll tell you what *is* boring," he said as he bit into a scone. "The clothes you're looking at. I didn't know there were still stores that sold things my grandmother used to wear."

She sighed. "I know. That's why we shop here. No one else carries these relics." She rolled her eyes. "My aunt likes to keep me firmly in the past. I'm just lucky she can't find hoop skirts for sale anywhere close."

He looked at her speculatively. "There were some younger styles on mannequins on the floor we came in on. Why can't you look at some of those?"

"Oh, because my aunt…" Her voice trailed off and her blue eyes widened as she realized what she was about to say. He was right. Why couldn't she look at some more fashionable things? She'd fallen into the habit of letting her aunt dictate these matters to her. She sat up straighter. "What a good idea," she said, looking around for the attendant.

"You'd like to see something from our young adult collection?" the woman said when Kari rose and went across the room to ask. "Of course. Your aunt requested these more mature styles, and frankly we were quite surprised to see how young you were when you came in." She smiled and gave Kari a wink. "Don't you worry about a thing, my dear. We've got consultants who know what's hot. It will only take a few minutes to set it up. But we'll need some further measurements." She eyed the very conservative sweater set Kari was wearing. "And perhaps you'd like to go ahead and try on a few representative items, just to get a feel for the sort of thing that suits you.''

Suddenly a tedious task was becoming interesting. Kari felt as if she was going on an adventure. She looked over at the table and gave Jack a smile, then turned as two teenage girls came out from a side door with measuring tapes in hand.

''Would you like me to ask your young man to wait outside?'' the older woman said.

''Oh, let her boyfriend stay,'' one of the girls who had a name tag that read Sheena said, laughing.

''We won't be doing anything too risqué,'' Mae, the other girl teased, giving Jack the eye in an open, friendly manner.

Kari looked across the room at Jack, and he met her gaze with resignation, just barely shaking his head to let her know he wasn't taking all this too seriously. She laughed softly and lifted her arms so that the others could begin to measure her.

She assumed they would just get her height, her waist, and maybe her shoulders, but soon she began to realize they were pulling the tape around every part of her, one saying the measurement while the other wrote down the number, and she began to feel a little more self-conscious.

''Get the breasts,'' Sheena called out to Mae in what Kari thought was an unnecessarily loud voice. ''Take a deep breath, honey, and push your chest out. If you got 'em, flaunt 'em, I always say.''

Mae pulled the tape tightly around the relevant items. ''And you got 'em, honey.'' She called out a number that made Kari blush, followed by, "Woo-hoo!"

Her cheeks were hot. She glanced quickly over to see how Jack was taking this and found him staring relentlessly at the wall. At first she was hoping he hadn't been paying attention, but then she noticed the twitch at the corner of his mouth and realized he was working hard trying not to laugh. And that made *her* laugh.

Moments later she was behind a folding screen that had been set up for her, trying on clothes the likes of which she'd never seen before, with a lot of help from Mae and Sheena, both clucking over her like a pair of bantam hens.

Jack waited restlessly, wondering what he had put in motion here. From where he sat he couldn't see much, but he could hear a lot of disjointed comments, and he had to admit they were making him curious to see the finished product.

"No, honey, you don't wear a bra with that. The point is to look sexy. Let it all hang out."

"Ooh, add three inch heels with ankle straps..."

"I know it seems tight. Here, Mae and I will help pull it on. If we all three shove at once..."

"Oh, those cranberry hot-pants are fabulous on you! Come on, try this black metallic net top with them."

The outfits sounded intriguing. The only problem was, Kari wasn't coming out from behind the screen to show them off. Every now and then he could hear her soft voice in a demurral of one kind or another.

It was pretty obvious the clothes were a little far out for her at this juncture.

"Ohmigod!" Sheena cried at one point in a piercing voice that could have cracked open glaciers. "Look how cool she looks in the green velour spandex capri leggings with the see-through crop top!"

"Oh, yes! Eat your heart out Britney Spears!"

Jack reached out and poured himself more tea. As visions of Kari braless and in metallic spandex filled his head, his mouth seemed to be getting drier and drier, and at the same time sweat was popping out on his forehead. He pulled out a handkerchief to mop his face before he realized what was going on, and he had to shake his head, embarrassed for himself. His imagination was running wild. If she didn't come out from behind that screen soon, he was going to have to get up and go take a walk around the building.

"Ready?" she said at last, and he looked up to see her look out shyly, then emerge in a long, slinky dress that glittered like Las Vegas and clung like a second skin. "What do you think?" she asked, looking at him hopefully.

Oh, Baby! was what he thought. But he didn't say it. "Very nice," he said. "It's…ah…very nice." And he started doing some shallow breathing in order to hold off a meltdown as she walked slowly before him, turned and started back.

"You hate it," she said accusingly.

"No." He gave her a strained smile. "No, I definitely do not hate it. But I don't think you'd better buy it."

"Why not? Doesn't it look good?"

"It looks too good." He gave her a wistful look. "I'm supposed to be protecting you. I don't need the extra risk factor."

She paused, looking worried, then noticed that his eyes were dancing, and immediately she laughed. "You're bad," she said, waving a finger at him. "You are very, very bad."

He grinned at her and she went back behind the screen, changing into her own clothes and joining him again, despite the urgings of the two girls to try a few more. Rock music was blaring from the speakers now, and young women came dancing out in one fashionable outfit after another.

Kari leaned close and whispered, "My aunt won't like this," to Jack.

"Maybe it's about time she let you pick your own clothes," he murmured back.

She nodded. "Of course it is. I know it. The whole world knows it. Now how do we tell her?"

She went ahead and ordered a few items to be sent to the house for her to try on later. Jack watched her and liked what he saw—liked it too much. Her look, her scent, the sound of her voice—everything about her was turning him on in a way that reminded him of his teenage years. Uncontrollable lust wasn't a pretty thing and he wasn't crazy about it in any case. He liked control, liked to think he could manage himself and events around him. But for some reason the attraction he was experiencing with this young woman was like nothing he'd ever known before.

Forbidden fruit, he told himself. That had to be it. He knew he couldn't touch her so the need to touch her was building like a summer storm inside him. If he didn't watch out, he might become the most dangerous thing she faced in her daily life. And he was the one who was supposed to keep her safe.

To keep her safe. The words went straight into his soul. That was his job now. Suddenly he wondered if he was taking it seriously enough. She was quick and bright and self-assured, but there was a vulnerability that surfaced when he least expected it. And whenever he saw that, something in him responded and he wanted to pull her close and make sure no harm could touch her. But that was mostly a man-woman thing. Was he ignoring the most dangerous aspects of this project? Was she in real jeopardy?

"So what is next on the royal agenda?" he asked as they waited for the attendant to finish the tally and present the list of outfits that would be delivered the following day.

"The parties, of course."

"Why so many parties?"

She gave him the impish smile that always made the corners of his mouth curl into a responding smile despite all his best intentions. "To get me married. I'm supposed to try out all these men. They'll be bringing them over in herds."

His smile faded as the horror of the situation finally became clear to him. Summer at the Roseanovas was going to be a regular marriage market. She was going to be auctioned off to the equivalent of the highest bidder. This might be what royalty routinely did, but it sounded barbaric to him.

"And at some point you'll choose which one will be your husband?" he asked, frowning at her.

"Well, the duchess will choose. She will decide who is the most suitable."

He was speechless. How could she be so casual about it? He was outraged himself, and ready to threaten bodily injury to any man who got too close to her.

"But it doesn't really matter," she told him reassuringly, putting a hand on his arm as though she sensed his agitation. "I'm not marrying for love. It's my duty."

Her duty.

He pictured a gray-haired geezer with a lecherous grin taking this lovely young woman in his arms, kissing her, taking her to bed…and his stomach churned as adrenaline raced through his system. He wanted to hit something—preferably the jaw of the disgusting mythical bridegroom.

He cleared his throat, forcing back his natural reactions and attempting to maintain his cool in any way that might be possible.

"When do they start bringing them in?" he asked, hoping she didn't notice how strained his voice sounded.

"Who?"

"All these eligible bachelors they are going to be parading in front of you in order for your aunt to make her choice."

"Ahh." She nodded wisely. "Actually, the first dinner is tomorrow night."

He squared his shoulders as though preparing for an onslaught. "Okay," he muttered to himself. "No problem."

She made a face at him, but then continued on. "We'll start small. There will be three or four of them at the first dinner. But don't worry. My aunt has assured me these men aren't very important. We have invited them as a courtesy, so they will feel they've had their chance. But they won't be considered in the end."

"'Had their chance'?" He looked at her quizzically.

She laughed and preened. "Of course. I'm quite a prize, you know." Grinning, she made sure he understood she didn't take it all so very seriously. "I don't mean personally, of course. I mean what I represent."

But *he* meant personally. She was very much a prize. She was beautiful and lively and carried herself with a natural nobility that couldn't help but shine through. Any man would be lucky to get her hand in marriage.

So why was there a knot forming painfully in his gut? It made no sense. He tried to tell himself that things might get easier once the men started hanging around. At least her mind would be occupied. Yes, that was it. Get her busy. Then things would get back to normal.

But what was normal? The way the allure of her

perfume got caught in his head? The way her face haunted his dreams? The way he felt her presence beside him even when he didn't turn to look at her?

Maybe normal wasn't so safe, after all.

Jack was sometimes disconcerted by Princess Karina and her candid reactions, but when it came to his job as head of security of the estate, he was confident of being on solid ground. Here, he knew what he was doing. With the approval of the duchess, he ordered new security fencing, a new alarm system for the house proper to be turned on between midnight and six in the morning, and a cell phone for Kari.

The cell phone arrived the morning after their department store expedition. On his way to deliver it to the house, he found Kari sitting with a book in the very elaborate rose garden. The Roseanovas, he'd learned, used the rose as the symbol of their royal house. The rose garden was laid out as a map of Nabotavia, with paths standing in for rivers, making a maze. Kari was sitting where the capital, Kalavia, would be. The huge rose bush covered with deep red roses was supposed to stand for the castle where her family had lived since the Middle Ages.

She was a vision in the early light, with sunshine streaming through her hair and her face still a little sleepy as she looked up to greet him. He held out the cell phone.

"What am I supposed to do with this?" she asked, holding it between her thumb and forefinger as though it weren't clean enough to touch.

He maintained his composure, though she looked pretty comical. He'd promised himself he wasn't going to fall for her charms any longer—or at any rate, he wasn't going to let it show when he did feel that warm curl of attraction unfold in his chest. That always looked so doable when he was in his own apartment, preparing his plans. After all, he'd fulfilled tougher assignments in his time. But when he came face-to-face with her, plans tended to crumble.

He had accompanied her back from the showroom display the previous afternoon, only to find the duchess waiting as they walked in, a suspicious look on her face as she watched their interaction sharply. They were a bit later than expected, and he could understand her concern. But he'd quickly assessed the situation and engaged the duchess in conversation, keeping a cool head despite the fact that they were smuggling in popcorn for the duke.

The princess had told him about the popcorn as they were leaving the department store showroom, making their way back downstairs in the elevator.

"My uncle loves it," she'd explained. "And my aunt forbids him having any. She's very strict about his diet, you know. And she has some sort of idea in her head that popcorn is bad for his digestion."

"I'm sure she's only looking out for his best interests," he murmured, though he wasn't sure of it at all.

"Possibly," she responded breezily. "But I think he deserves a treat now and then, so I get him popcorn whenever I can sneak it in."

The elevator doors opened and she began to lead him toward the counter that stocked such things.

"It's got to be the candied kind," she said instructively. "And it's got to be in a vacuum pack, because of the smell, you know. That always gives it away. And if the duchess catches me..." She made a face that revealed dire consequences in a comical fashion.

He had to hold back a grin, but he allowed himself one comment as they came to a stop at the counter and began to wait for service. Looking at her sideways he murmured, "You're awfully sneaky, for a princess."

She laughed. "You don't understand royalty at all if you don't understand how sneaky the whole system is. To be royal is to put on an act. It's all a false front." She sobered, getting philosophical. "We have to try to be larger than life, because that is what people expect of us. If you just come across like an average, everyday person, people start to pout." She demonstrated, putting on a silly voice. "'What's the point? Who needs royalty like this?' I've even heard it said that the Russian revolution became possible when the people saw Czar Nicholas and realized he was just a scrawny little man. People began to say, 'Well, who's scared of a czar like that?'"

He had to laugh at her antics. She was absolutely adorable. He stood beside her and watched as she purchased her popcorn, feeling a wave of affection for her that made him groan inside.

But once they were home and faced with the suspicions of the duchess, he worked quickly, distracting her attention with a list of security concerns for her to deal with while Kari gave him a wink and slipped away, suitably disguised popcorn in hand, to visit her uncle.

There was no longer any doubt in his mind—the princess was a very special person. And she deserved every bit of creative protection he could manage to provide. Equipping her with a cell phone was only the beginning as far as he was concerned, and here she was, resisting his efforts.

"Hold it like this," he said firmly, taking her hand in his and showing her how to hold and flip it open, then immediately pulling away when he realized he was back to treating her like a pretty girl rather than a royal presence. Somehow he had to get it through his thick head that there was a wall between them, a wall he would be a fool to try to breach.

"The best thing to do would be to wear it at your waist. See, it has a clip at the back. That way you'll always have it with you."

"Is that really necessary?" she asked, still looking as though she would just as soon drop it in the nearest waste receptacle.

"It's just another element in our security system. It's meant to make you safer, to give you a means of communication in case anything should happen." He frowned at her. "What is your hesitation? Every girl your age in the civilized world carries one of these around with her at all times. Most wouldn't know how to function without one."

She shrugged, not at all convinced. "You still haven't told me what I am supposed to do with it."

"It will come in handy if you need to get a hold

of help quickly. And you can use it to call your girl-friends.''

She raised her head and met his gaze honestly. ''I don't have any girlfriends.''

She said it without irony, without bitterness, without guile. So much so that for just a moment he thought she must be joking.

''What are you talking about? I've never known a woman who didn't have friends. It's part of their nature.''

She shook her head. ''Not me,'' she said simply, a certain sadness shadowing her blue eyes.

He was still having trouble with this concept. ''What about those two girls who were over swimming with you the other day?''

One perfectly sculpted eyebrow rose. ''Were you watching us?''

''No, of course not.'' Suddenly his ears were burning again. What was it about her that made him do that? It had never happened with anyone else. ''But I did happen to see them with you,'' he went on doggedly, hoping she didn't notice the color of his ears.

She shrugged. ''I'd never met them before and I doubt I will see them again. I believe they were just passing through, though I didn't really get a chance for a good talk with either one of them. Besides, it would be too risky to make friends with anyone in the Nabotavian community. Too much chance for treachery.'' She shook her head. ''I'm quite serious, Jack. I have no real friends.'' A slight smile played at the corners of her mouth. ''I did have an imaginary friend when I was little. I called her Bambi.'' She looked at him quickly, wishing she could take that admission back. She'd never told anyone before. Was he laughing at her?

No. His eyes were stormy, and he was filled with a certain anger as he contemplated what her life must have been like growing up this way. What sort of archaic and sadistic system kept this lovely young woman from living a normal happy existence like that of others her age? What had all this protection and elitism done to her? And was it really worth it? No girlfriends, no life... And he thought *he'd* been deprived growing up with no family. Suddenly he realized that they had more of a common bond than he'd ever thought possible.

"Well, you should have a friend," he said tersely. "In fact, I'm going to look into getting you one."

She stared at him for a moment, and then a smile just barely crinkled the corners of her eyes. "I didn't know you could order them up," she said. "Darn! I would have bought one years ago if only I'd known."

He didn't smile. In fact, he felt more like he needed to hit something and he turned away from her.

But she followed, putting a hand on his arm to get his attention back. "You mustn't blame us for our old-fashioned ways," she told him earnestly, seemingly reading his mind and knowing how he felt about her upbringing. "We've lost our country. We hang on to as much of our traditions as we can manage. They are all we have left."

Of course. He knew that. Swallowing hard, he forced himself to remain casual and even attempted a look of unconcern. She had her life and he had his. There was no reason their two existences should touch in any form whatsoever, except in the most professional way.

It wasn't easy to figure out why she had this ability to reach in and take hold of his emotions the way she did. Regardless, he couldn't let it show. In fact, it was probably time he put some actual distance between them, before the duchess walked out into the yard and saw them talking. Instinctively he knew she wouldn't like it at all.

He looked down at her hand on his arm, and she removed it, flattening it against her own chest. His gaze followed, and for some reason he couldn't pull away. Her fingers were slim and tapered and looked beautiful against the lightly tanned skin showing above the scooped neck of her lace-edged top. The vision she made touched him, made him yearn for her. He ached to take her in his arms.

Their gazes met and held for a long, quivering moment. But as each second ticked away, he was gathering the strength to do what had to be done. And finally he gritted his teeth and looked away.

"I've got to get going," he said gruffly. "You practice with that cell phone. Get used to it. It won't hurt you to join the modern world, at least this little bit."

When he looked back, he found her smiling at him in a way so wise, he immediately feared she could read his mind and knew exactly what he was thinking. But she didn't make any comment, turning from him, picking up her book from the bench and starting toward the house.

"I guess I'd better get going, as well. I have a lot

to do to prepare for this evening." She turned back and gave him her impish grin. "Tonight is the night. Madam Batalli is due soon to do my hair. Let's hope she manages to make me beautiful."

He nodded, mixed feelings grinding through him. "So you're pretty excited," he noted dryly.

"Well...sort of." She shrugged. "This is the first step toward the beginning of the rest of my life. I'm about to launch, in a way. The way debutantes are presented. The way young ladies were introduced to society in the old days."

He nodded again, fighting the impulse to say something to her. It would be better to let her go, he knew. He had no business imposing his thoughts. But he just couldn't leave it alone.

"Princess..." He stopped, shoved his hand in his pocket and turned to go, then turned back. "Listen, be careful, okay?" he admonished awkwardly. "I mean, about the man you pick. You deserve the best. Don't settle for anything less. Okay?"

She nodded, her eyes filled with the bright light of the sun. Suddenly she took a quick step toward him as he turned to go again.

"Wait...look," she said, making an elaborate show of attaching the cell phone to the waist of her slacks. "Here, I'm putting it on. I'll be so much safer now, in case I get lost in the woods or fall down a rabbit hole or something like that."

She looked up expectantly at him, like a child hoping for approbation. Then she sighed, as though she realized she was going over the top.

"I appreciate the attempt to protect my interests.

Really, I do. And I'll wear this faithfully as a token of my appreciation.'' She gave him a sharp salute, like a cute toy soldier at attention.

He bit back his own grin. "Thank you, Princess," he said formally. "Just remember to use it if you do find yourself in any sort of sticky situation."

"Oh, I will," she said. Her eyes lit up as she thought of something. "And once I memorize your number, I'll be able to call you anytime, day or night."

He hesitated warily. "Sure, if you're in trouble…"

"How about when I'm lonely?" she asked softly, her eyes luminous. "Or when I need some good advice?"

His face darkened. "Princess…"

"I know, I know," she said lightly, turning away and starting for the house again, book in hand. "I'm being frivolous." She looked back at him from the doorway. "But I'm going to memorize your number, anyway." She put her hand over the cell phone at her waist and added, in a voice just above a whisper, "I think you would make a wonderful friend."

And then she was gone.

His heart twisted inside him, and he stood where he was, muttering every obscene swear word he could think of—anything to keep from feeling the emotions she triggered in him.

Chapter Five

Looking the current crop of suitors over later that evening, Jack tried to remain objective. If he was going to provide Princess Kari with the proper level of security, he had to understand what was going on around her. Emotions couldn't be allowed to cloud the issue.

He stayed in the background during dinner, blending in with the help and watching as the duchess and her guests were served an elaborate meal at the long, dark dining table. Huge candelabras lit the high-ceilinged room, casting shadows on the richly flocked walls. The duchess sat at the head of the table. Seven adults as stiff and mannered as she was were scattered up and down each side, and four young men sat between them, attention all on Kari, who sat at the other end. The conversation was polite. It seemed almost formulaic to Jack, as though each was reading from a script she'd learned for the occasion.

But that all changed as the party finished dessert and retired to the game room for liqueur in tiny crystal goblets and more animated conversation. The adults sank into plush chairs around a large felt-covered gaming table while the younger ones gathered at the far side of the room, encouraging Kari as she played a few light tunes on the piano.

All four of the young men were very handsome, though one had a dissolute look and another seemed bit vacant. They were all much younger than Jack had expected. There were no old lechers looking for a young bride here tonight. That should have been a relief, but somehow it didn't help. He still hated seeing them crowd around her, vying for her attention.

"She looks like Scarlett O'Hara at the barbecue," he muttered to himself as he stood, feeling restless, in the dim light of the patio off the gaming room.

A chuckle nearby told him he'd been overheard and he turned to find the duke coming up to stand at his elbow. "You hit the nail right on the head," the duke told him softly, nodding. "Look at her. Isn't she the most fetching thing you've ever seen?"

Jack turned back to take in the scene reluctantly. The older man's admiration was well-founded. Kari was wearing a violet dress that fitted her bodice like a glove, then flared out at the hips into a filmy cloud of transparent fabric that played teasingly about her long, lovely legs. It was one of the dresses they had looked at the day before, so he assumed her choices hadn't been completely vetoed by her aunt. Kari's hair was swept up into a cascade of curls that was old-fashioned but appealing, and her face was shining with joy. Jack had never seen a woman look lovelier. He was afraid to leave his gaze on her for too long, afraid a part of him would begin to burn inside. She was just as her uncle said, completely fetching.

The young men circling her were another matter, and the duke filled him in on their identities himself.

"Now Leonard Bachman's lineage goes back to the Holy Roman Empire," he noted, pointing out one with a decidedly superior look to him. "Eugene is one of the British royal cousins," he added, nodding toward the blonde. "Not very bright, I'm afraid, but awfully good at cricket. And Nigel is a very nice lad. I once thought I was in love with his mother."

That got Jack's attention. He smiled at the duke, really looking at him for the first time and realizing how sweet he looked for a man his age. His hair was either very blond or had turned a stunning shade of white, and was combed back in a debonair style that belonged to swells of another age.

"The one to watch out for is that redhead," the duke continued, unabashed. "He has a very wild reputation among the younger crowd. I don't like the look of him. He brings to mind a young Oscar Wilde."

Jack nodded. "I'd been thinking something along those lines myself," he murmured.

"Good. I'm glad you have an instinct for these things." The duke nodded his handsome head ap-

provingly and patted Jack's shoulder. "I trust you'll
be keeping a close watch on our young lady. And
making sure none of these young swains get too fresh
with her?"

Is that what I'm supposed to do?

He only thought the words, but the question was a
good one. He knew he'd been hired to keep Kari safe,
but no one had been very clear on the extent of that
safety. Was he expected to make sure she didn't risk
breaking her heart? Was that a part of it all?

I hadn't understood that morals patrol was part of
the job.

Again he didn't say the words aloud but thought
them as he muttered something agreeable instead.

The duke went on telling him anecdotes about each
of the guests. The stories made Jack grin, and even
laugh once, and he wondered why the man was being
so friendly. He'd met him on occasion for only a few
moments at a time, but he was acting as though they'd
known each other for years. Something told him Kari
was the reason. She must have mentioned him to her
uncle. But what could she possibly have said that
would make the man feel as though they were practically comrades?

He threw a casual glance in her direction. She was
laughing, and the redheaded gallant was leaning toward her, touching her cheek, saying something that
was obviously impertinent. Every muscle in Jack's
body clenched. The young man drew back his hand,
and Jack slowly, purposefully, made himself relax.

Whether the family wanted morals patrol or not, his instinct was doing the job on its own.

"Well, I suppose it is time to honor the scene with my royal presence. Frankly, I'd rather stay here chatting with you, but duty calls." The duke gave him a sad half smile. "As for my young lady, I'm sure you'll take good care of her," he said with a wink, then straightened his tie and set off to join the party.

Jack frowned, not sure what the duke had meant by that. Suddenly Kari's head lifted and her gaze met his across the room. She caught him off guard, and her smile shot straight into his heart. He saw a connection in it, a recognition that he should be in on her private joke. Suddenly he knew exactly what she was thinking just as though she'd whispered the words in his ear. She was having the time of her life but it wasn't serious—he wasn't to take it as such, and she wanted him to laugh at it with her. She wanted to share her joy with him.

He couldn't let that happen. The emotion knotting his stomach had nothing to do with humor. Telling himself to ignore this wasn't working. He was caught in a maze with no way out. Unless he took the initiative and made an escape route for himself. He took a deep breath. Time to do just that. Moving farther back into the shadows, he pulled out his walkie-talkie and called Greg Pinion, his right-hand man. It was time to hand the rest of the evening over to someone better equipped to handle the torture. He was getting out of here. A man could only take so much.

* * *

Kari bit her lip. Jack was leaving. She could tell. As he briefed Greg, she could read the signs. He was transferring the assignment and heading off to do something else.

Suddenly the delight drained out of the evening. Much of what she'd been doing had been an act meant to impress him. It had been fun, even thrilling for a time. There was certainly nothing boring about being admired. But more than that, she'd wanted Jack to see her as the center of a lot of male attention. She was sure that was a wicked thing to want, and now she was pretty sure it had backfired on her.

Of course, she was being foolish and she knew it. Much as she liked Jack, much as her pulse rate quickened whenever he was near, she knew there was no future for the two of them. She had gone through periods of feeling rebellious in the past, but that was all over now. She knew her destiny. She was going to marry and do her duty. She owed that to her parents and to her culture. In another few weeks she would be engaged to be married to an eligible nobleman of her country.

She caught her breath. That thought always made her feel as though she'd just fallen off a very high ledge. Married. How could she be married when she knew nothing—nothing at all—about men? She couldn't help being terrified of the whole situation.

"This isn't about love and kisses and romance," her aunt had told her often enough. "You don't need to know anything at all about men. That's irrelevant. This is about duty to your family and your country.

It is about securing the future of the nation, helping your brothers to make it stronger. That is what you were born for.''

Of course she would do her duty. But other girls got to date and flirt and have fun with boys they didn't intend to marry...didn't they? She was never going to be allowed to live like a normal person, but this one little thing...this friendship with a man who made her feel light-headed...couldn't she at least have this? Was that so horribly selfish?

She looked around at the faces of her admiring new acquaintances. Every one was well connected, handsome, charming. The man who would be picked as her spouse would be a lot like one of them, only probably a bit older—someone stable, ready to settle down, but of the right family and with the right connections. Someone eminently eligible for her hand, just as these were. Perfect for her.

This was what she'd been waiting for all this time. The days of being stuck with the old folks were gone. She was now allowed, even encouraged, to have fun with young men. She ought to be like a kid let loose in a candy store.

And yet compared to Jack these handsome suitors seemed colorless and uninteresting. It was lovely to be the center of their attention, but she'd had enough for tonight. She was ready to give up this pretense for the time being. She wanted to see Jack again. Ached to see him.

The handsome redhead was leaning close, murmuring sweet nothings meant to make her swoon, but she wasn't really listening to him. Her heart beat faster as she made her decision. Yes, she was going to see Jack again. Tonight.

Jack leaned back into the pillows he'd piled against the arm of the couch and yawned, turning off the television. Dressed only in slacks, he'd been flipping channels and finding nothing that could hold his interest. It was late. He'd been putting off going to bed but he'd waited long enough. Maybe now he would finally be able to fall asleep without thinking about...

He swore softly. No, he wasn't even going to let himself *think* about thinking about her.

This fascination with the girl was completely unlike him. He'd spent most of his life as a man's man, more at home with a group of buddies than with a girlfriend. He figured that was because of the way he'd grown up, in foster families and group homes, usually with a boy or two for a pal and very little contact with the opposite sex.

That had all changed in high school, of course, but though he'd dated a lot of pretty girls, he'd been more at home with his football teammates. Girls made him nervous. He just didn't understand what they expected. It seemed to him they said one thing when they really meant something else, and his head would swim as he tried to figure out what was going on.

The mystery girls posed faded as he hit his twenties. He even had a few fairly long-term relationships. But somehow his heart had never been truly touched. And when each relationship ended, he didn't look back with any sort of remorse. Women were easy to get when you wanted one.

The single thing he did regret, however, was letting a woman mess with his life in a way that might turn out to be downright disastrous. It had already played havoc with his career. Now he was waiting to see if his partnership with Lucy Dunlap—and the mistake of trusting her—had turned his future to dust. By the end of the summer he would know.

There was a sound at his door, a knock so soft, at first he wasn't sure if he'd imagined it. He frowned. Someone at his door at this time of night could only mean trouble. Assuming it was one of the guards, he rose from the couch and sauntered to the door, ready to point out that a call on his cell phone would have been a quicker way to get his attention.

But he never made that little speech, because he pulled the door open and found Kari on his doorstep.

"Hi," she said in a voice meant to be muted to the outside world. "Let me in, quick."

Stunned, he did as she asked and immediately regretted it.

"You can't be here," he noted sternly, lurching back. "Don't close that door."

But she did, snapping it shut before he could reach it and then turning to grin at him. "Shh!" she said with a finger to her lips. "No one knows I'm here."

She'd dressed herself all in black, from her slinky turtleneck sweater to her soft jersey leggings. Her face was scrubbed clean of the makeup she'd worn earlier, and her hair was combed out and floating softly around her shoulders. Every time he saw her she looked more lovely than before. It was like a disease, and he was suffering from a rare and possibly fatal case of it.

"Why didn't Greg stop you?" he demanded, glowering at her. "He's supposed to be guarding the back of the house."

"I waited until he was distracted by something and I sneaked right past him," she said proudly.

"If he's that easy to fool, I'll have him fired in the morning."

Her eyes widened in horror. "Oh, no, don't do that. It wasn't his fault."

"If he can't do his job…"

"No, don't you see?" She gave him her most irresistible impish smile. "It isn't that he's so bad at what he does. It's all because I'm so good at what I do. You can't punish him for…for that…"

Her voice faded at the end because she'd finally taken in the condition she'd found him in. Her gaze trailed over his naked torso, lingering on the hard, chiseled muscles of his chest, his strong upper arms, the washboard panels tapering into his slacks.

"Oh, my," she said in a tiny voice.

He groaned and turned, rummaging in the couch, throwing pillows aside, looking for his shirt. "This is exactly why you shouldn't be here," he warned, finally spotting it and yanking it out to slip into. "You have no business coming to my apartment," he went on as he hastily worked with the buttons. "If the duchess knew you were here, she'd pack you off to a convent.''

"I had to come," she said in a strangled voice. She took a deep breath, then blinked hard a few times, regaining her equilibrium as he covered up his gorgeous flesh. "I need your help."

"What for?"

She looked at him expectantly, throwing out her hands. "Aren't you going to ask me to sit down?" she said. "Isn't that what people usually do when someone comes to visit?"

He hesitated. He wanted her out of there as quickly as possible, but he knew darn well she wasn't going to budge until she'd said her piece.

"Have a seat, Princess," he said at last, biting out the words crisply. "And tell me what you need help with."

She sat gingerly on the edge of the couch, while he dropped to drape himself casually on the opposite arm, as far from her as he could possibly get. She noted that, then looked around at the simple living room, the small kitchen just off it, the hallway toward the bathroom and bedroom. Bookcases lined the walls, though there wasn't much filling them. The old security man had lived here for years, but when he'd left, he'd taken a lot of the furnishings and Jack hadn't replaced them with many personal items. She knew he was only here for the summer, but she was disappointed he hadn't set out more clues to himself and his life. She wanted to see what he liked to read, maybe some pictures of friends, a favorite item from his past. But there was nothing she could put her finger on. Jack seemed to enjoy being an enigma.

"It would be so much fun to have a place of my own," she said wistfully. "A place I could decorate my own way and have people over to visit." She sighed. "Don't you just love being on your own?"

He shook his head, his mouth twisted cynically. "The female urge to nest," he said. "It seems to be universal." His mouth hardened. "But this isn't getting us any closer to your problem."

"My problem?"

His brows drew together. "You said you needed help."

"Oh. Of course." She smiled at him. "This is going to sound a little strange. But it's actually quite serious. You see, I need to learn how to kiss."

He choked, which set off a short coughing fit.

She leaned toward him. "Do you need a good thump on the back?" she asked hopefully.

"No!" he said, leaning away from her. "I'm fine. It's just..." He coughed one last time and shook his head, looking at her in wonder, squinting as though that would help him see her better. He manufactured a glare, just to show her he was serious. "What did you really come here for?"

She thought for a second or two, then shrugged. "The kissing thing was it."

He groaned and she added defensively, "I thought it was a good idea. I think you ought to teach me how to kiss. Because I really need to know."

He looked at her uneasily. She was so pretty, so

impossibly desirable, and so completely unaware of the danger she could have been in. She shouldn't be saying things like this to a man like him. Still, he wasn't totally convinced that she wasn't pulling his leg.

"Why?" he asked suspiciously.

"Don't you think it's something I ought to know?" She didn't give him time to answer, talking fast. "I've been taught how to dance, how to make small talk, how to drive a car. Don't you think it would be best if I were taught the intricacies of kissing? After all, I might be doing quite a lot of it this summer."

He stared at her for a moment, then turned away, muttering something she couldn't quite make out. So she went on making her case.

"You know that song, 'Sweet Sixteen and Never Been Kissed'? You could change the lyrics for me." She let out a tragic sigh. "Bitter twenty-two and never even been touched by any man." Her face changed and she almost smiled. "Except you, of course," she added, dimpling playfully.

"Me?" His head whipped back and he stared at her. "What are you talking about?"

"When you came into my room that day. Remember? You grabbed me." She sighed dreamily. "It was great. I think about it every night before I fall asleep."

"Well, don't." Rising, he began to pace the room, running his hand through his thick hair as he did so. This was no good and could get a lot worse. He had to play it carefully. "Just forget about it."

She just smiled and he stopped before her, arms folded across his chest.

"Are you seriously trying to tell me you have made it twenty-two years without once being kissed?" he demanded.

"Of course."

He shook his head. "How could that be?"

"I've never been left alone with a man. I always have someone with me." She shrugged. "That makes it rather difficult to fool around."

He shook his head again, hardly knowing whether to believe her or not. The experience she was portraying was so far removed from that of the average young woman her age, it seemed like a fairy tale. But then, she *was* a princess, wasn't she? So fairy tales would seem to apply.

"There was no point in letting me date," she went on helpfully. "I always understood that perfectly well. Why should I go out with boys who have no chance of ever marrying me? What if I fell in love? It could be disastrous."

"It still could be," he noted softly, staring down into her beautiful eyes.

She held his gaze, head high, but there was an excitement quivering deep inside her. "I think I can handle it," she told him quietly.

He shook his head slowly. "You don't know what you're talking about," he told her. It took effort, but he forced himself to turn away and begin pacing again. What was he going to do with this girl?

She watched him, a slight smile tilting the corners

of her wide mouth. "You're probably right," she said. "But don't you see? That's just the problem." She waited a moment, but he kept pacing, hands shoved deep into his pockets, so she went on. "It occurred to me tonight that I really haven't had enough experience in handling men. I need help. My older brothers aren't here, so I can't turn to them. My uncle is hopeless and the duchess would just snap at me." She turned her palms up appealingly. "So I have no one else to turn to but you."

He stopped, turning to look at her. It was still an improbable scenario. Beautiful young princess appeals to lonely cop to teach her to kiss. No one else would believe it. Why should he?

"What happened tonight?" he asked her softly, his eyes searching hers, looking for evidence that there was more to this request than she was admitting to. "Did one of them try to…?"

"No, nothing like that," she said quickly. "But I want to be prepared, in case anyone ever does 'try' anything. I need to know what's possible, what to look out for. How can I defend myself if I don't understand what's going on?"

She was getting through to him. She could see the tiny seeds of doubt beginning to germinate. She was starting to persuade him to see it her way. Time to get back to the heart of the matter.

"But what I really need to know," she said softly as she looked up into his eyes, her own wide with innocence. "What I really need is lessons in how to kiss."

"Oh, no," he said, backing away from her. "There's no reason in the world you need to know how to kiss."

She rose, following him. "You wouldn't want me kissing some count or earl and having him think I'm just a callow schoolgirl who doesn't know what she's doing, would you?"

He stared at her, once again wary of being fooled by her innocent act. "Oh, come on, Princess. I imagine that's exactly what they want. Someone who's completely…untouched." He choked on the phrase and his mind was flashing words like *pure* and *virginal*. He had to turn away so she wouldn't see what that did to him.

"If you won't teach me how to kiss, I'm going to have to look for someone who will." Her eyes narrowed speculatively. "I suppose I could ask Count Boris," she mused.

He turned back, frowning fiercely. "Who the hell is Count Boris?" he growled.

She smiled at him. "The duchess's younger brother. He's coming for a visit soon. I haven't seen him since I was about ten years old, but I remember that he seemed very handsome to me at that time."

She waited, watching the conflicting emotions play in his dark gaze. It was all so blatant she was almost embarrassed. But she knew instinctively that she was never going to get anywhere if she left it up to him. So here she was, doing the best she could manage.

"What exactly is it you want to know about kissing?'' he asked her, though she could see it cost him something to give in, even to this extent.

"I thought maybe…you could show me how?''

"Oh, no.'' He shook his head firmly. That was obviously out. Completely out. Wasn't going to happen.

"Well, at least you could give me some advice,'' she said sweetly.

"Advice?'' He looked relieved. "Advice. Sure. Why not? I'll give you some advice.'' He pointed at the couch. "You go sit down. You make me nervous standing so close. And I'll think up some advice to give you.''

She went back to the couch obediently, slipping out of her shoes and curling her legs up under her, looking very comfortable. He stood on the other side of the room, arms across his chest, gazing at her.

So now he was supposed to be some sort of expert. What the hell did he know about man-woman relationships? Poor thing, she didn't realize he was the last man she should be asking. You didn't get great helpful hints from someone who had failed at what you were aiming at. He could tell her what to avoid. He could tell her relationships weren't worth the effort. He could tell her not to trust anyone. That was pretty much the way he handled his own life. But somehow he didn't want to steer her in the same direction. Maybe she would be lucky. Maybe she would find something good in this rotten world. He didn't want to ruin that for her.

"Okay, the first thing you have to realize is that as a woman, you have all the power.''

"The power?" She blinked in surprise. "How can that be? Men are bigger and stronger and..."

"Sure, men who are thugs can overpower you physically anytime they want to. But that's not the sort of power I'm talking about. With any normal man, it's going to be up to you to control things."

He stepped closer to where she sat, the subject suddenly as engrossing to him as it was to her. And that was odd because he'd never thought this through before. But now that he was considering it, there seemed to be a lot of theory floating around in his head, and he had to wonder how long that had been going on.

"You're beautiful, appealing and very sexy," he told her earnestly. "Men are hard-wired to react to that sort of thing. They can't even help themselves. Around a female like you, they're helpless."

She bit her lip to keep from snickering at him. Men helpless—what a concept. If men were so helpless and easy to control, why wasn't Jack kissing her right now? She took a deep breath and waited, listening intently.

"Which makes them very dangerous. Because a helpless man is going to feel cornered and is likely to do something stupid. So you have to learn to treat every man with a firm hand, but with some compassion at the same time." He frowned, shaking his head. "Is any of this making any sense?" he asked her. "What I mean is, you have to learn to play your cards very close to the vest, and to be aware of what kind of reaction you are getting at all times."

She laughed softly. "Oh, Jack, you're the quintessential law enforcement officer, aren't you? So suspicious of everyone."

He didn't welcome her comment. "Look, you asked my advice."

"I did, indeed," she said quickly, looking suitably abashed. "Sorry. Please continue."

He made her wait a beat or two, then went back to pacing as he warmed to his subject. "Okay, talking specifically about the prospective husbands—well, put it this way. Any guy worth his salt is going to want to kiss you. It's up to you to hold your kisses safe. They're worth a lot. It's up to you to decide who you value enough to squander them on."

She dangled a foot over the edge of the couch. "What if I decide I want to kiss them all?" she asked breezily.

"No!" He stopped short, frowning at her. "No, because a kiss isn't just a kiss."

She gazed at him quizzically. "Then what is it?"

He thought for a moment, wanting to get this right. "It's an invitation. It's a promise. It's a way a woman opens the door, even if just a tiny crack, into her soul."

She gasped softly. She hadn't realized Jack could be so poetic. "Just a little kiss can do all that?"

She watched him wide-eyed. She was beginning to understand what he'd meant. She thought she felt a little of the power he'd been talking about in the way she could feel that he was drawn to her. It was intoxicating. It made her think things possible she might not have dreamed of before coming here. What if…?

She rose and planted herself in his pacing path. He turned and almost ran into her, reaching out to steady her with his hands on her shoulders.

"I think you should show me that kiss now," she said softly.

The look that flashed in his eyes might have been alarm, or it might have been something more dangerous. She wasn't sure. At any rate he turned her down.

"I don't want to kiss you," he said flatly.

Her lips tilted at the corners. "Yes, you do," she said daringly. "I vote we be honest about this. Okay? You want to kiss me. And I very much want you to. So what's the holdup?"

He thought about turning away, but it had become impossible now. She was too close. Her scent was filling his head. And he couldn't seem to pry his fingers off her shoulders. But he had to try to keep this thing from steering off the cliff.

"Princess…"

"Scaredy-cat," she taunted softly, smiling up at him.

She felt so fragile in his hands, so deliciously pliable. Light as a breeze, sweet as a rose.

"No," he said, as much to himself as to her. Hell, he was strong enough to resist this. This was nothing. "No, we can't do this."

"Jack," she said, cocking her head to one side and looking deep into his eyes, "if you won't kiss me, someone else will be my first. Please be the one."

Resistance crumbled abruptly, and something close to pain was squeezing his heart. "Well, maybe just a small kiss,'' he heard himself saying. ''A quick one. Just so you see…''

Oh, who was he kidding?

''No hands,'' he warned, releasing her shoulders. ''No touching.''

She clasped her hands behind her back and he held his hands in fists at his sides. She leaned toward him, and he leaned toward her. She closed her eyes.

The first thing that surprised her was that his lips were so soft. He was a hard man with a hard body and she'd expected hardness. But no. His lips were as soft as kitten fur and smooth as whipped cream. And yet it wasn't comfort she was feeling. Heat curled through her like smoke, fire began to lick in her veins, and every nerve ending seemed alive and aware as they had never been before.

She kept her hands clasped behind her but she arched toward him, instinctively wanting to feel her breasts against his chest. At the same time, her lips parted slightly and the tip of his tongue touched them, and then he jerked back, breathing quickly and scowling at her as though he was very sorry for what he had just done.

''I didn't mean to do that,'' he began, then swore softly, turning away.

She was standing there, all dewy and luminous, her lips still parted, and he knew she wanted more from him. And there was no denying every part of him wanted the same thing—and more. He grimaced, feeling like a man drowning in golden nectar, a man who had to claw his way back to the surface. But he was a man who usually did what he had to do, and he managed. And when he could breathe normally again, he turned on her sternly.

"Look, I think it's time for some plain talking. You want truth? Let's both face some facts." He pointed at her almost accusingly. "You are a princess. You're royal. You were born to be one of the elite." He ran his hand distractedly through his hair, setting it on edge. "I come from the opposite end of the spectrum. I'm nobody. I come from nowhere. I've got nothing."

She winced, hating that he was talking like this. "Jack…"

"In fact, the only reason I was available to take this job was because I'm on suspension from the police department. I'm being investigated. I might get fired."

That was news to her, and she didn't know what to say. Still, she made an attempt. "Jack, that doesn't matter. I can tell what kind of man you are."

"Can you?" He shook his head. "Sometimes I'm not too sure about that myself. You know where you come from. There are books full of your genealogy. I don't know anything about my background except that there's got to be an Italian in there somewhere. I was raised without roots, without history, without money." *Without love,* he could have added, but he would rather have died than say it. "We can't…I mean, you know there is no chance for there to be anything…"

Kari rolled her eyes toward the heavens and turned

with a sigh, slipping back into her shoes. She'd tried. But now she was getting angry.

"Save your breath," she told him evenly, tossing her hair over her shoulder as she stepped past him. "I'm not a foolish child. And I'm not falling in love with you. You take all this much too seriously." She stopped at the door, looking back. "I just wanted to learn how to kiss. That's all."

Pulling the door open with her head held high, she disappeared into the night.

Jack stared into the dark for a moment, then strode after her. He didn't say a word as he passed her, but went straight to where he knew Greg was standing sentry duty and engaged him in conversation, giving Kari cover to get into the house without being seen. And when he finally got back to his apartment and closed the door and leaned against it, closing his eyes and laughing softly, he realized one thing—she'd taken his lesson about power to heart, and she was a quick study. Maybe he wasn't going to have to worry about her social relations after all.

But there was something else, something that made his laughter fade quickly. He knew it was going to be a long and sleepless night as he fought his body every minute.

Chapter Six

"Stay away from Jack Santini. He's no good for you."

Kari looked down at her perfectly polished pink fingernails and chewed on her lower lip while she waited for Mr. Blodnick to finish his tirade.

"If I'd known something like this would happen, I'd never have hired him. But I darn well should have known, shouldn't I? After all, I knew all about his suspension from the department. That was over a woman, too. His partner, of all things. I should have kept that in mind..."

"Mr. Blodnick," she said quietly, having had her fill of his overreaction. "If you please."

"Oh." The man calmed himself quickly. "I'm sorry, Your Highness. But when you ask me a question like that—"

"Mr. Blodnick, nothing has happened. No transgressions are being contemplated. All is well.'' She pulled her robe more tightly around her shoulders. She was dressed for a swim, but had stopped by to ask him questions because she knew her aunt was out of the house at the moment and wouldn't notice. "I merely asked you to tell me what you know of Mr. Santini's background. Idle curiosity, nothing more. There is no need for you to let it upset you so.''

"Your Highness…Princess…are you sure? Because if I were to be the cause of ruining your life, I would really feel bad about it."

Kari laughed and reached out to squeeze the man's hand with a great deal of affection. "I'm sure. Now tell me. What did Jack Santini do to deserve a suspension?"

He looked like a man being tortured on the rack. "Have you talked to the duchess about this?"

"Be serious. I'm the one who told you to hire him, aren't I? Do you think I would give her a chance to tell me how wrong I supposedly was?"

He shivered at the thought. "I wouldn't think so."

"Exactly. So come on, mister, spill the beans."

He shifted in his seat and looked very uncomfortable at being in the position of having beans to spill. "I don't really know the details. And I've only heard of it in the most general terms, so…" He coughed. "Well, from what I've heard, he let his feelings for his female partner get the better of him and ended up getting blamed for something she did."

His words cut into her hopes, but she wouldn't allow him to detect that. "I see," she said, all calm and casual.

"There is an ongoing investigation. And a hearing in late August. If he's cleared, he'll be back on the force in no time. But if the board rules against him..."

She nodded. "Was there a romance involved?" she asked, hoping her voice didn't betray how much this was costing her.

He hesitated. "You got me. All I know is, women are always falling for Jack. So I imagine it was something like that."

She smiled, rising from her chair. "Thank you, Mr. Blodnick. You've been very helpful."

He grimaced. "And you won't tell the duchess?"

Her short laugh held a trace of irony. "I'll never lie to her. But I certainly won't volunteer anything unless I'm forced to by circumstances."

"Good." He shook his head with a worried frown. "I'd hate to see him lose this job. I think his being employed here will look good to the board. Just in case he needs that extra boost. And him getting fired would look very bad."

There was no doubt about that.

But Kari left the man's office with a heavy heart. She had absolutely no right to be jealous, but human emotions were difficult to control, and she was feeling rather glum at the moment.

It had been almost a week since that night in Jack's apartment. He'd been avoiding her ever since. She knew he was right to do that. She knew that it was best for them both. They should just stay away from each other.

She'd been wrong to go to him that night. She'd been even more wrong to insist he teach her how to kiss. And yet, whenever she thought about it, she couldn't really regret it. It made her smile when she remembered how he'd tried to avoid kissing her. It made her gasp to remember what his kiss had felt like.

Still, he was right. They couldn't be together. There was no place for them as a twosome in this world. She needed to set her sights on her future, on the man who would be her partner as she returned to her country and began to serve her people the way she had been born and bred to do.

And there was a new angle. The more she was finding out about his situation, the more she realized that his position was quite precarious and could be threatened if anything happened to cause him to lose this job. Just from things she'd heard and things he'd said, she was putting two and two together and getting a rather scary scenario. It would be cruel to him to pursue him in any way. So she just had to stop it. Now, if only she could stop thinking about him as well.

Stepping out onto the veranda, heading for the pool enclosure, she stopped for a moment. She could see Jack in the distance, standing in front of the five-car garage, talking to one of his agents. At the other end of the property, she caught sight of her aunt, giving orders to one of the gardeners. Chin high, she ignored them both and went straight toward the swimming pool, dropping her robe on the deck and diving in without hesitation. She swam ten laps before she paused.

There, she thought. That's better. But she knew she was fooling herself.

She didn't know enough about men. That was the crux of the issue. Her brothers were always so far away, and her uncle was so often remote. After dressing, she quietly slipped down to the rooms the duke kept for himself and knocked on the door. Once he bade her enter, she opened the door and looked in.

"Hello, my favorite uncle," she said with forced cheer. "I've come to ask a favor. I need you to tell me something." She smiled at him tremulously. "Will you tell me about my father?"

Jack was carrying a ladder into the library the next day when he realized Kari was already in the room, sitting at a desk, books and papers spread out all around her.

"Hi," she said, looking up cheerfully.

"Oh." He stopped. He wanted to work on some wiring that had come loose in the alarm system, but he could do that some other time. "Sorry, I didn't know you were in here. I'll just go and let you have some privacy."

"No need to do that. I just came in here to transcribe some of my notes. You won't be bothering me." When he still hesitated, she flashed him a look of pure exasperation. "Don't worry. I'm not going to try and corner you to get another lesson in kissing or anything like that.'' Her mouth tilted in a slight smile. ''That was childish. Immature. Manipulative. And I'm sorry I did it.''

He turned to look at her questioningly, and her smile got rueful. ''Oh, rats,'' she said. ''That's a lie. I'm not sorry at all. But I know I should be, and I'm trying hard to be. It's just that, so far, it's not working.''

He couldn't help it—she made him laugh. And she made him want her with a yearning that was quick and deep and stronger than it should be. For just a moment he let himself dream, looking at her as she sat at the desk, her blond hair in disarray, her lacy blouse twisted, her short skirt revealing long, lean and gorgeous tanned legs that seemed to draw his gaze straight up to where it didn't belong.

What if she were just an ordinary woman? What would he be doing right now? Flirting, no doubt about it. Giving off signals. Looking for response. Wondering how long it was going to take to get her into his bed. Anticipating how sweet it was going to be to taste her nipples, how his hands were going to explore until he'd found all her most responsive secrets, how he would awaken her to things she'd never known before. At the same time, the need for her would build and build in him until it was almost unbearable, until he would slide into her body and take her all the way, and finally find a relief for himself so intense it would almost bring him to tears as her soft cries of pure wonder and delight filled his ears.

Whew. He blinked hard, forcing himself back to earth and looked at her quickly, hoping his thoughts hadn't been too obvious. But she didn't look alarmed. She was saying something about the notes she was compiling. He cleared his throat, still standing before her with the ladder in his hand.

"Notes?" he asked, scanning the books and papers she had spread out before her. "Are you giving another speech?"

"No. Thank goodness." She sat back in her chair, crossing her long legs and looking completely comfortable with herself and her circumstances. "Didn't I tell you about my three main goals for my summer?"

"No," he said, forcing his gaze to avoid looking at those lovely legs. "I don't remember anything like that." But then, he could barely remember his name at this point. He looked at the ladder he was holding. It took a moment to recall why he had it with him, but once he did, he went into action, setting it up along the far wall, greatly relieved to have found something to do besides standing there drooling all over the sexy princess who was supposedly in his care.

"Okay. I'll tell you now." She put down her pencil and rose, walking over to where he was beginning to climb up the ladder. "I have three big goals for my summer. Number one is to write a book about my mother's life. A biography. I'm actually using that as a device to explore a history of my country."

He was up high now. She looked very petite and

young from his upper perch. Still, he had to admit, the way she carried herself gave her a presence you just couldn't deny. No one would have to be told that she was royal. And from up here, her breasts looked so damn appealing...

"You remember that she was killed by the rebels when we escaped from Nabotavia. She and my father both."

He nodded as he reached into the vent with pliers. Maybe he could cut into a wire and get electrocuted, thus putting himself out of this misery. But misery wasn't really the right word for what he was feeling. Sweet torture was more like it. And if he were honest, he would have to admit it felt dangerously delicious, despite everything.

"That's why I want to find out all that I can about her and write it down. Before it's too late and everyone forgets."

He finally realized what she was talking about, and that caught him up short. Here she was discussing her murdered parents and he was off in fantasyland instead of giving the subject the respect it deserved. He quickly vowed to mend his ways.

"What about your father?" he asked by way of catching up as he threaded the wire into place.

"He's had a ton of books written about him," she said, wandering down the wall of floor-to-ceiling stacks and pulling out a book about the king, waving it at him, then shoving it back in. "But my mother hasn't. I want to use her story to fill in the lives of women of her time." She looked into space. "I want to write a memoir about Nabotavia, about how it used to be before the revolution. My uncle is helping me with it, but I'm also interviewing some of the older servants to get anecdotes from their lives, as well as some of my aunt's friends when they come to visit. I really want to get a lot of different perspectives." She turned back to see if he was still paying attention.

"How are you doing it?" he asked, snapping closed the opening he'd been working on.

"I have a little recorder I use. I just turn it on while talking to people. Then I transcribe the tapes later, go through and edit, pick out the parts I want to use. My uncle looks my work over and makes suggestions."

"Really." He was impressed, now that he was paying enough attention to understand what she was doing. His image of a pampered little princess whiling away her time eating bonbons and accepting flattery from the huddled masses was fading fast.

"Once I get it into a form I can live with, I'll have a few other Nabotavians of the old school look at it and tell me what they think. Eventually I hope to have it printed up and put into the national library."

"I think that's great." And he really meant it. She was quite ambitious in her way, and he admired that.

"Do you?" She glowed under his praise. "I hope it turns out to be something Nabotavia can be proud of. I live for my people, you know."

He winced. She'd finally hit a note that sounded sour to him.

"What are your other two goals?" he asked her,

changing the subject as he started back down the ladder.

She threw out her hands and dazzled him with a bright smile. "Number two is this—I want to learn to cook."

He stopped at the bottom to look hard at her. "Why would you want to learn that? You'll always have others to do that for you."

"That's exactly why I need to know. I don't want to be a silly princess who couldn't feed herself if anything went wrong." She slipped back onto the library table, sitting on the end, swinging her legs. "Things happen, you know. And I want to be prepared. And I don't want to be someone who gives orders and has no idea what others have to do to perform chores for her." She chuckled softly. "Besides, I don't think you've ever been at the mercy of a royal chef. It can be quite an experience. If he goes on a kick, say he reads that anchovy paste on everything brings good luck or something like that, you might just be faced with a week's worth of inedible food. I've seen it happen. Not a pretty sight. It's smart to be prepared for the worst."

He nodded, bending down to pack his gear into a toolbox. "And number three?" he asked.

"And number three, of course—I have to get married."

Straightening, he looked at her and nodded again. "Of course." His fingers curled around a pair of pliers. "How are things coming on that front?"

"Well, our next dinner is Friday night. The more

serious candidates are due to arrive. I'll be wearing one of the dresses I chose the other day and having my hair done in a special new style in the afternoon.''

''You're having your hair done again?'' It seemed to him that the hair dresser was a daily visitor lately.

She laughed at his naiveté. ''I have to look my best, you know. Madam Batalli will be coming to help me before every party, and especially before the ball in August.''

''Really.'' He frowned thoughtfully, still holding the pliers. Madam Batalli was an older lady, almost elderly. One would think a princess would want to try some younger style ideas. ''And all to catch yourself a royal husband.''

She went perfectly still, staring at him. ''You don't approve.''

He lost it. If he'd only stopped for a moment and thought. After all, he was no one but an employee. He had no call to react the way he did. But by the time that realization had taken place in his mind, it was too late. The words were out.

''Damn right I don't approve. This is like some ritual out of the Dark Ages. This is like selling your oldest daughter to the highest bidder. I wish you'd reject it. I would think that a woman like you, with all you've got going, could tell them all to go to hell and walk out of here.''

Her head jerked back as though he'd slapped her. ''Gee,'' she murmured. ''Don't hold back. I wouldn't want you to feel as though your opinion had been overlooked.''

He grimaced, rubbing his neck. "Sorry," he said gruffly. "But you asked."

"Indeed I did." She gazed at him seriously. "So I take it you don't think much of royalty."

"I didn't say that," he replied. "It was useful once. I think royalty was nice while it lasted, but it's had its day and should get off the stage."

"But what if the people of a country want their royalty?" She shook her head. "It's a double-edged sword, you know. The people are locked into their traditions, and we're locked into providing something they want to have. I was born into a certain situation and I owe it to my people to fulfill my role."

He was beginning to wonder how he'd ended up in this position. It certainly wasn't a comfortable one. "Your people kicked you out," he noted dryly.

She whirled to face him. "No they didn't. That was only one small segment that took over. And now they are gone and the people seem to want us back."

"So you think you're really going back?" He'd heard something along these lines, that Nabotavia had held a plebiscite and the royalty was being begged to return. Funny how once he had the name of the little country in his mind he seemed to be hearing about it everywhere.

"Oh, yes. That's what this is all about. That's why I have to marry right away. By the end of the year, we'll all be going back. And it looks as though my oldest brother will be crowned as the new king."

Jack frowned, wondering what that would be like. "Does he want that?"

"Well, of course. It's his destiny. His destiny and his duty." She saw his skeptical look and went on a bit defensively. "We were all raised with a sense of what our duty is, and I think that is a good thing. It helps to raise us above selfish concerns. Don't you find you become a better person once you commit yourself to a larger cause? Especially when it involves doing good for others."

"I suppose so," he murmured doubtfully, but memories were floating into his mind, reminders of when he'd been a Navy SEAL and how he'd felt when he'd been active in the police force. She was right. He'd always been happiest when working for a bigger issue.

"You know about that," she said, as though she'd read his mind again. "You're a cop."

He glanced her way. "Yes, I am."

"Do you still feel a sense of duty to the police force, even though you're under suspension?"

His gaze hardened. He wished he hadn't told her about that. Still, it was hardly a national secret. "Sure I do," he said speaking curtly. "The situation I'm in was my fault, not theirs. I could have avoided it if I'd been smarter."

"From what I've heard, you were protecting your partner."

He groaned, looking away.

"I also heard your partner was a woman." She stopped right in front of him. "Did you love her very much?"

He looked down into her eyes, wondering why she

was pushing this. "Princess, look. I know you live in a fairy-tale world, but most of us have to deal with a more mundane existence. Things don't follow the usual story lines."

She cocked her head to the side, regarding him with a piercing look. "There's nothing fairy-tale about my world. Just the names. Otherwise, it's very boring."

"So is being a cop. The cop shows on TV—they hype that up to make a good story. Real life is not like that."

"So you're saying you weren't madly in love with her?"

He almost had to smile at her dogged determination to get the straight scoop. "No, I was not madly in love with her."

He was in pretty heavy duty "like" there for a while, but he didn't have to tell her about that. Liking Lucy, feeling a lot of sympathy for her, all that had clouded his thinking at the time. And that was what ought to remind him of how important it was to keep a distance. He'd just about ruined his situation on the force by letting personal relationships get in the way of his duty. He'd be damned if he would let that happen again.

He started away, hesitated for a moment, then turned back. "I probably should warn you. I've ordered that the dogs be let loose to roam the estate during the night."

Her head came up and she stared at him. "The dogs?"

"Yes. The Great Danes that are kept in the kennel

behind the garage. I found out they were originally purchased to be guards, but no one ever followed through and actually trained them. So I've hired a trainer who says they can start right away.''

She nodded thoughtfully, her eyes cool as she gazed at him. "I see. So…is this because you want to guarantee I won't come visiting you at night?'' She cocked an eyebrow in that royal way she sometimes had. "Are these vicious beasts supposed to take the place of poor old Greg who 'couldn't do his job right'?''

He made sure that his expression didn't change. "It has nothing to do with that, Princess,'' he said.

"Really.'' She didn't believe him for a moment. "I see. Well, thank you for warning me. I'll be on my guard.''

He turned, ladder in hand, and almost ran into the duchess as she made her regal way into the library. She nodded to him curtly, then frowned as she looked at her niece.

Kari sighed. She would have liked a bit longer with Jack, but now he was out the door and there was no hope of clearing the air between them. And she was left with the duchess looking as though she'd walked in on a romantic tryst.

"Oh, Aunt, don't look so cross. We were only talking.''

The duchess looked skeptical as she dropped into a chair at the library table. "I'm not sure it was such a good idea to hire that man,'' she fretted. "I now hear that he has had problems in the past and is currently under suspicion of using his status as a police officer to cover criminal activity.''

"He's completely innocent," Kari blurted out, then regretted it as her aunt looked at her sharply.

"How on earth would you know that?"

"I just…Mr. Blodnick told me," she improvised quickly. "And he has known him for years."

The duchess drew her head back and narrowed her gaze. "I think I'd better have a talk with our Mr. Blodnick."

Kari's heart was in her throat. "You're not going to have him fired!"

Her aunt turned and stared at her. "Why is that so important to you? What's going on here?"

Kari knew she'd made a big mistake reacting as she had. Now she was going to have to summon all her acting powers if she was going to turn this around. Very carefully she composed herself and managed to look casual and unconcerned, if slightly offended. "Oh, Aunt, there's nothing going on. Heavens, I've got enough on my mind right now. But I wouldn't want anyone fired just because rumors circulate about him." She smiled at her older relative. "And I wouldn't want anyone fired because of me."

"It wouldn't be because of you."

Kari threw out her hands. "Why not? He was hired because of me."

"True." Her aunt seemed at least partially mollified. "Anyway, I don't have time to deal with that this week. I'm going to be traveling to San Francisco overnight. I'll be back in time for our Friday night dinner, however." She sighed, looking at Kari. "But you mustn't worry your head about these things. You just concentrate on readying yourself for matrimony, my dear. And the return to Nabotavia. Those are the only things you need to think about." She rose from her seat at the library table.

"By the way, my younger brother, Count Boris, will be arriving next week. He'll be staying with us for the rest of the summer." Her smile seemed to hold much pleasure at the thought of her brother arriving. "He was quite fond of you when you were a child. I hope the two of you will still get along."

Kari was breathing a sigh of relief and hardly paid any attention to this talk of Count Boris. "I'm sure we'll do fine," she said airily, not giving it a second thought.

"Oh, yes," her aunt agreed, smiling as though she was quite pleased at the prospect. "I'm sure you will."

Chapter Seven

Princess Kari was in the kitchen the next morning when she got a surprise. Something was making a funny electronic sound, and she looked around the room for the source, then put her hand over the small bulge at her waist, realizing it was her cell phone. She'd been faithfully wearing it around for days without having any action at all.

"It's ringing!" she cried to no one in particular, since the room was empty except for her. She'd never had a real cell call before. Grabbing it, she flipped it open and said, "Hello?"

"Hi, Princess. It's Jack Santini."

"Jack!" Her heart leaped. "This is so exciting."

"What's wrong?"

His voice was filled with concern and she laughed. "No, it's just that you're my first call. Ever."

"Oh." He seemed to find that puzzling, but not interesting enough to pursue. "Are you alone?"

"Yes."

"Good. I've got some news. You know your hair appointment for this afternoon?"

Now it was her turn for puzzlement. "Yes."

"I'm afraid Madam Batalli can't make it today. I've found you someone new."

Kari frowned. "But I've had Madam Batalli since I was sixteen."

"All the more reason to try someone else. Don't worry. She's fine as far as security goes. Her name's Donna Blake. She's actually a good friend of mine."

"Who you just happened to have handy." Kari wasn't sure she liked this. "You haven't fired Madam Batalli have you?"

"No. Of course not. I can't do that. I just…sent her on a little vacation."

"What?"

"Never mind that now," he said quickly. "I just wanted to warn you. I think you'll like Donna. Here's her number." He rattled it off rapidly. "You can call her to confirm. She's waiting to hear from you."

"Jack…"

"Trust me. You'll like her. I've gotta go."

She clicked off, slightly confused but at the same time strangely happy. She'd had her first cell phone call and she liked it. Jack had actually called her.

"May it be the first of many," she declared out loud.

But the more she thought it over, the more her spirits drooped. Maybe this wasn't such a good thing after all. As she analyzed it, she began to think she might just know what Jack was doing. He figured if he contacted her by phone, he wouldn't have to risk any more face-to-face encounters. He was already calling out the dogs at night to keep her away and now he was using the phone to fend her off in the daytime. She had a sudden epiphany. Women used the phone to draw people closer. Men used phones to keep people at a distance.

So that's your angle, she thought, pursing her lips. Well, we'll just see about that Mr. Jack Santini. We may just have another card up our royal sleeve.

Pulling the cell phone off her waist, she pressed in his number, tapping her fingers against the counter while she waited for him to answer.

Jack hung up, letting out a long breath. She charmed him every time. She was so open, so innocent, so lacking in guile of any kind. It gnawed at him that he was now manipulating her as baldly as any woman had ever tried to manipulate him in the past. In some ways you might almost say he was sending in a spy. Well, not exactly a spy, but something almost as repugnant.

But that wasn't really fair. Donna was no spy. She was a darling and Kari needed a friend. As soon as he'd decided to try to provide her with one, Donna had leaped immediately to mind. He and she had both lived in the same group home the year before he'd joined the Navy. Though she'd been a few years younger, they'd struck up a friendship that had lasted ever since. They had even shared an apartment for a while, platonically, when he'd first been discharged from the Navy and she'd just finished cosmetology school. Donna had a basic decency and bright view of life that Kari might respond to. In his experience she had warmed the heart of everyone who had ever met her.

Kari had said she had no friends. Well, Donna would be a friend if Kari would let her be. He couldn't go so far as to manipulate the way the princess would feel about Donna, but he was pretty sure he knew how his old friend would feel about the princess. He couldn't imagine anyone not loving her at first sight.

Still, his conscience was nagging at him a little. The duchess wouldn't have approved, but she was out of town for the day—or Jack would never have tried to pull the switch this way. Maybe he was just being selfish, bringing in one of his own personal pals to be buddies with Kari. It was probably unethical as all get-out, but it wasn't necessarily illegal. He sighed. It was hell getting involved in a personal relationship, but here he was, stuck in one, whether he wanted to be or not.

His cell phone rang and he reached for it automatically.

"Hello?"

"Hi," Kari said. "It's me."

"No kidding." He couldn't help but smile at the sound of her voice.

"Since we're now in cell phone contact, I thought we ought to work on secret signals," she said pertly.

That opened his eyes. "What?"

"In case I get kidnapped or something. If I have my cell phone with me I could give you a call and tell you my location using code words if we have them set up ahead of time."

He had to smile at her enthusiasm, but at the same time he knew he had to squelch it. "The first thing that any competent kidnapper will do is strip you of your cell phone."

"Oh." She paused, but not for long. "Well, what if they're not competent? I'll bet the Sinigonians wouldn't have thought of doing that."

His brows drew together. "Who are the Sinigonians?"

"The people who kidnapped me before."

Shock catapulted him up off his chair. "You were kidnapped before? Why didn't anyone ever tell me?"

"Oh, it happened so long ago. It was no big deal."

No big deal. He swore softly, shaking his head, and when he spoke again, his voice was like struck steel. "Where are you?"

"I'm in the kitchen. But I'm very busy..."

"Don't move. I'll be there in less than a minute."

She sighed happily as she closed her phone and put it back at her waist. Sometimes things really did work out for the best. By the time he arrived in the doorway of the kitchen, she'd barely gotten back to work on the counter she was cleaning.

He stepped into the room and looked around suspiciously. The huge light-filled space gleamed with copper-bottomed pans and stainless steel appliances. Only the island butcher-block counter was a mess, covered with flour and the remnants of dough that Kari was cleaning. He looked at her as though he could hardly believe what he was seeing.

"Where is everybody? Do they leave you alone in here?"

"Very funny." She went back to scrubbing down the wooden counter. "Cook and I have been making the dough for dinner rolls. She's gone to take her midday nap, and I'm cleaning up."

"You're kidding."

"Why would I kid you about that? Here's the dough." She pulled out a large flat tray to show him the saffron-colored dough waiting to rise. She displayed it with all the pride of a creator. "Isn't it beautiful?"

"It's beautiful all right. I just can't believe…" But he looked at her flour-dredged hands, then her wide eyes, and cut his comment off without completing it. "So you're cleaning up."

"Yes," she said defiantly, going back to her scrubbing. "I'm cleaning up." She glanced up at him from under her tousled hair. "What do you think? That I'm making this up?"

"No. No, it's just that…well, you're a princess. You don't need to do this."

"Oh, yes I do," she said calmly. "Besides, I like doing it."

He watched her for a moment. Right now she could

have been any young woman in any kitchen in the country, doing chores that needed to be done. But no, he took that back. She was much more beautiful than any other young woman of his acquaintance, and the way she was scrubbing that counter, putting her whole body into it, she was also more hardworking. She was a puzzle. And she was also the cutest thing he'd ever seen.

He shook his head over her desire to play scullery maid, but decided to let it go. "Okay," he said crisply, crossing his arms at his chest. "Tell me about this kidnapping."

She shrugged, pushing back a stray hair with the back of her hand. "I told you it was long ago. No one has ever said anything about it to you because for the most part, I'm sure, they've all forgotten about it. It wasn't very significant, even at the time." She went back to scrubbing. "I was about thirteen, I think." She rinsed out a rag and began to wipe the counter dry. "It was the Sinigonian family. They are kind of the Keystone Kops of our homeland. They are always trying to gain advantage over the other factions, but they are just so incompetent. It never works out for them." She rinsed the rag again, hung it to dry, and turned to face him. "They only took me to their house in Santa Monica. My brothers came and rescued me before anything really happened."

Jack frowned. The entire operation sounded wacky, but he was considerably less alarmed than he had been when he'd first heard about it. He slumped onto a stool set at the counter, casually draping across it. "They didn't hurt you?" he asked her.

"Oh, no, not them." She plunked down on a bar stool next to the one he was sitting on, drying her hands on her apron. "They were very sweet to me, actually. Now the Davincas…that's a different story. You don't want to be kidnapped by them. They're a bunch of thugs. They took one princess and held her for ransom for weeks. They kept her in a vegetable cellar. It was horrible."

Jack shook his head. The Nabotavians seemed to be particularly enamored of nabbing royalty. "Were your kidnappers asking for a ransom?"

"Oh, no." She wrinkled her nose. "They only wanted me to marry their son, of course."

Jack gave her a look of outrage. "At thirteen?"

"The old-fashioned types think that's a great age. Catch her while she's young and too naive to complain, they say." She shrugged. "But they needn't have worried. My aunt has kept me young all these years." Her tone wasn't exactly bitter, but it was the closest thing to it. "I've been carefully nourished and coddled. I'm still like a thirteen-year-old girl. If you know what I mean." She held back her laughter. "Of course, I have recently been taught something about kissing, but not nearly enough to put me in the experienced category. Do you think?"

He avoided her gaze and steeled himself. He would be damned if he was going to let himself blush again. She was taunting him and he knew it. She was also tempting him, and he wasn't going to take the bait.

"But that is neither here nor there," she admitted breezily. "The most important thing—of supreme importance—is to keep the blood line pure." She gave a casual wave in the air. "After all, succession and all that."

He risked a look at her and then he couldn't look away. She was wearing tight, patterned leggings he'd seen her eyeing at the showing the other day, along with a lacy white blouse and the red rose pin that symbolized her royal house, a pin she always wore. Her clear skin seemed to glow with a magic sheen that made him want to kiss her. But then, just about everything made him want to kiss her.

"I suppose that's pretty important for keeping the royal boat stable in troubled waters," he said gruffly, trying to keep his focus.

"Absolutely." She smiled, knowing he understood. "That's what happened to my darling duke. He's my father's half brother, you know." She dropped her gaze as she went on. "He was illegitimate. His mother was a lady-in-waiting to my grandmother. And that means he can never be king, you see." She looked up again. "My brother Marco will succeed. And whoever marries me will be very highly placed in the hierarchy of things." She sighed. "Unless, of course, they try to marry me off to a royal from another country. Then who knows what will happen to me?"

He wasn't going to say what he thought of this whole rotten system. She was wedded to it and obviously thought she could live with it. He got crazy thinking about how easily she could give her life up to others to guide for her. He had moments of a wild fantasy of carrying her off himself. Luckily he wasn't insane enough to think something like that might work. She was what she was and he was what he was.

"And never the twain shall meet," he muttered to himself.

"What's that?" she asked, but he shook his head.

"So tell me," he said instead. "What happened to these people? Did you have them prosecuted? Are they in jail?"

"Oh, heavens no. They're harmless little folks. We Nabotavians mostly take care of our own."

He had to look away and swallow hard at that one. Come on, come on, he told himself impatiently. Just because their system is nuts doesn't mean you have to fix it for them. Just let it be.

But he had to find out a few things. "So you're telling me they could still be out there, plotting to snatch you again."

She put her head to the side, considering. "Oh, I doubt that. From what I've heard they've given up on me long ago. They've already married their son off to some lower level princess."

"Uh-huh. Just how many princesses do you people have?"

"Oh, tons of them. At least, there will be when everyone returns. They're all cousins who married other cousins. You know how that goes. It's a mess, believe me."

His wide mouth quirked at one corner as he

watched her. "So that's your problem," he said dryly. "Ever think you people might need to bring in some fresh blood?"

She looked up at him and smiled. "Sounds like a good idea to me," she said softly.

He grimaced and went on. "From the briefings I've had, it's been my impression that the group called December Radicals is the one to look out for."

"Yes. They're the ones who killed my parents." She sat back, all smiles extinguished. "For a while they had all the power. But they've lost it over recent years, and they've been trying to get it back." She shook her head. "But there's no hope for them now. The country is becoming a democracy ruled by a constitutional monarchy. However, I suppose it's best to remember, as you were telling me the other night, that it is when people feel cornered and helpless that they are the most dangerous."

He nodded thoughtfully. It was a disturbing thought. From what she'd told him, he gathered that the Sinigonians merely wanted a bride for their boy. The December Radicals probably had something else in mind, like blackmail, ransom and revenge. The only thing he knew for certain was that he must never give them a chance to get their hands on her. Them, or anyone else who didn't have her best interests at heart.

Suddenly, inexplicably, he felt overwhelmingly protective toward her, and it was not on a professional level. It had everything to do with her huge blue eyes and the trusting way she looked at him and very little to do with a paycheck at the end of the month. He wanted her in his arms the way a starving man wanted bread, with a deep, primitive need that threatened to choke him.

And she seemed to sense that things were veering into forbidden territory, because she slid off her stool and made it clear that it was time for him to go. He got up more slowly, his inner turmoil not as easy to turn off once it had started simmering.

She looked about the kitchen, then set her jaw and faced him squarely. "I'm not going to fall in love with you, you know," she told him. "So you can quit worrying right now."

"All right," he said, because he couldn't think of anything else to say about a statement that so thoroughly took his breath away.

"I guess I'd better go give this friend of yours a call," she was saying, "if I'm going to get my hair done in time for the dinner tonight."

"Oh. Good." He stopped and faced her, reluctant to go anywhere she wasn't going to be. "Donna's a peach. You'll like her."

Kari took a deep breath and asked, "What is she to you?"

"What do you mean?" But he saw in her eyes what she meant. "Oh, she's a friend. We've been friends since we were kids." He wanted to reassure her, then realized doing that would only make things worse. "We both ended up in the same group home after bouncing around from one foster family to another. So we have similar backgrounds that tie us together.''

"Unlike you and me," she said, her eyes dark.

"Unlike you and me," he agreed, his voice rough.

Suddenly she reached up and flattened the palm of her hand to his cheek. "There's no one else like you," she said softly.

He ached to taste her lips. Reaching up, he covered her hand with his own, then took it and pressed a kiss into the center of her palm, his gaze holding hers, burning into hers. Something passed between them, some connection was made on a nonverbal level that made them both breathless. He dropped her hand and turned quickly, leaving the way he'd come, and she stood where she was, savoring the lingering sense of the kiss she'd captured in her hand.

What did it mean? She didn't know. She didn't want to know at this point. She only wanted to feel, not to think. Closing her eyes, she held her hand to her own face and smiled.

Then she remembered the telephone call she still had to make and her smile faded as she remembered this Donna person. She hated this jealous feeling she had. She'd had it about his partner and now she had it about his hairdresser friend. Mr. Blodnick was probably right—he was the sort of man who women fell for in droves. There were always going to be women around him. And it really had nothing to do with her. So why did it make her heart twist in agony?

* * *

Kari started out the hair session determined to dislike Donna, but in very little time she realized that was going to be an untenable position. Donna's dark hair was cut in a bob that left her with bangs barely revealing bright green eyes that sparkled with interest and the joy of life. She started right out acting as though she'd known Kari all her life, without a hint that she might in any way be in awe of royalty.

"Here's what we'll do," she told her new client once they were alone in Kari's room. "While I'm setting up my equipment, you go through your snapshots and other pictures for the last year or so and pull out any you find where you think your hair looked its best. Also, if you have any pictures from magazines, or whatever, of hairstyles you'd be interested in trying, get those out, too. Then I'll sketch out some ideas using your facial shape and your bone structure as a foundation. And then we'll see what we can come up with."

They spent the next two hours together, giggling over pictures, trying out various outrageous styles, then settling on something less flamboyant but very different from the style Kari normally sported. All in all, it was the sort of fun that Kari wasn't used to, and she had to admit, she had a very good time. She ended the session liking Donna a lot, despite her original reservations.

Still, she wondered about the relationship Jack and this woman might have had in the past.

"So you've known Jack just about forever," she said, being carefully casual, as they began packing Donna's equipment and implements away.

"Oh, yeah, we go way back," Donna replied, giving her a quick smile that revealed her understanding of how things were. She stopped and looked at Kari earnestly. "Look, hon, don't be embarrassed if you've got a crush on the guy. Not many girls who meet him can resist a bit of one, you know. He's so cute and so very, very manly." She gave her a wise and knowing look. "I know you know what I mean."

Kari couldn't help but smile. "How about you?" she asked curiously.

"Me?" Donna laughed. "He's like a brother to me. Do you have a brother?"

"Oh, yes. I have three of them."

"Then you know what it's like. In some ways we're almost too close. There's not enough mystery left between us. You know what I mean? I adore him, but not that way."

For some reason—maybe because she just wanted to so badly—Kari believed her. Just before Donna left, they had a last look in the mirror together, both nodding with approval. The "do" was sophisticated, yet young and lively, with curls cascading down one side of her head and small tendrils teasing her ear on the other side. Kari was excited. She felt like a different person.

"Oh, I hope you can come again sometime," she told Donna impulsively. "I mean, I love old Madam Batalli, but..."

"Don't you worry about the madam. She's on her way to the Caribbean."

Kari frowned. "Whatever do you mean?"

"Didn't you know? Jack got her a position on a cruise ship. Seems she's always wanted to travel and this is her chance. She won't be back until fall."

Kari stared at Donna. "Why would Jack...?"

"He didn't tell you?" Donna shrugged and smiled at her, then launched into a long explanation, talking so fast Kari could hardly keep up with her thoughts. "Well, here's the deal. Jack told me about your situation, how you have to marry some dude you hardly even know, because of your duty to your native country. And I really admire you for that. I know I couldn't do it. But he also told me that you have wealth and you are going to have power, but the one thing you don't have, because of your position, is friends. He said to me, 'Donna, every woman needs a friend.' And you know, he's right. It's genetic. It's born in us. But he said, 'You go be her friend, if she'll have you.' And I told him I'd give it a try. I'd have to see if we got along. And if I liked you." She grinned. "And I guess you could say I like you just fine." She shrugged. "So that's where we are. And if you decide you want me to come back, I'll sure do that. But it's up to you."

Kari didn't know what to think. She'd seldom met anyone quite this straightforward. "Is this sort of like hiring you to be my friend?" she asked warily.

Donna gave an explosive laugh. "No! You're hiring me to be your hairdresser. The friend thing comes free." Impulsively she reached out and gave Kari a hug. "Darling, I'd love to be your friend. And I'd love to be your hairdresser. But if this just doesn't work for you, I'll understand." She turned to go. "Just remember, anything you say to me will be strictly confidential. Even from Jack. It's part of the hairdresser's code." She laughed, and as Donna left, her heels clicking down the hallway, Kari smiled. That laugh was infectious.

"I may just have a friend," she whispered to herself in wonder. And that was fun. But the fact that Jack had done this for her was harder to think about. A part of her wanted to find the angle, wanted to puzzle out the reason he might have done such a thing. What did he have to gain? Was Donna here to watch her for Jack?

"Or is he just a wonderful, wonderful man?" In her heart she thought she knew.

Chapter Eight

The duchess hated Kari's new hairstyle. And she was furious to find that Madam Batalli was now working on a cruise ship. She'd come back from her overnight trip in a hurry to make it to the evening festivities, and she'd been presented with a fait accompli that she didn't agree with at all. She knew whom to blame.

"That Jack Santini man has got to go," she fumed. "I've been suspicious of him for quite some time and now he's overstepped his authority. We never should have hired him. I want him fired right away."

The atmosphere was electric with her criticism, but Kari's response stopped all that. She stood listening as her aunt went on and on, detailing how Jack was to be fired, and at last, when her aunt paused for breath, she made her statement.

"No."

The word echoed through the drawing room. The duchess stopped and stared at her. Tim Blodnick, who'd been jotting down notes on just how the firing was supposed to go, gaped at her, as well.

"I don't want him fired," she said calmly, facing them both with quiet dignity. "I think he's done a wonderful job and I want him to stay."

The duchess regained her composure quickly. "My dear young lady," she said icily. "I don't think you know what you're talking about. Older and wiser heads will make these decisions for you. We're only thinking of your own good, you know."

Kari shook her head stubbornly. "I'm sorry, Aunt, but I won't hear of it. I'm over twenty-one and can make my own decisions now. Jack Santini stays."

The duchess fussed for a few more moments, but her tone was unconvincing. She'd been shocked by what Kari had done, but it was obvious she'd known it would happen at some point and she was beginning to be resigned to it. After all, truth to tell, Kari *was* the princess, and for the first time in her life, she was pulling rank. She'd never even dreamed of doing such a thing before. But it felt very natural now that it was done.

And though she wouldn't stop and frame the thought in full, a part of her knew instinctively that Jack had become more important to her than just about anything else.

In some ways the evening was like a rerun of the week before. There was a new cast of characters, but the circumstances were similar. Even the conversation seemed like something heard before. But the dinner was up to the usual high standards. Kari made sure Jack got slipped a roll, one of the ones she had helped Cook prepare that morning, then waited for his verdict. When he gave her a surreptitious thumbs-up, she put her nose in the air with a "See? I told you so," display of hauteur. But when she peeked at him again, she caught him laughing, and that made her smile, as well.

Unfortunately, that incident provided the most interesting moment of the evening. This group of aspirants was older, more world-weary and not as prone to the sort of giddy courtship practiced by the younger set. Still, from the look in each eye she could tell they mostly thought she would make a pretty fine plum to be baked in their particular pie.

But that wasn't likely to happen. She found them all pretty boring. One was a future minister of health for the upcoming administration. Another was destined to manage the educational system for the newly reorganized country. A third was a sort of a rich playboy who had been married to a film star but was recently divorced. He drank too much wine and fell asleep during dessert and had to be carried to the couch.

The remaining gentlemen talked about politics and business—things she knew were important—things she knew she was going to have to begin paying attention to herself. But she didn't relish the idea. She was still too young for this, darn it! She needed a little more time. She needed some other sort of man. Someone like…

No, she wouldn't say it, not even to herself. But her gaze sought him out. He was standing in the shadows at the far end of the room, talking to her uncle, as he often did. But his gaze met hers immediately and he acknowledged her with a very slight, almost imperceptible wink. He looked as strong and handsome as any statue by Michelangelo, and it was quite clear his main object in life, at the moment, was to make sure she was safe. Watching him, she felt a surge of something hot and sweet that filled her soul, and her heart fluttered in her chest.

I'm in love, she thought. And the shock of it shivered through her.

No, she couldn't be. She couldn't let herself be.

Yes, I'm in love. I'm in love with a man who stirs my blood and is living his life to make mine better. A man who takes time out of his day to think about finding me a friend. How could I not love a man like that?

She'd told him only that afternoon that she wouldn't fall in love with him. But what else could she have said? If she'd told him the truth, he would have been worried about things he didn't need to worry about. Because it was clear as glass to her that she would do her duty, no matter what. Falling in love wasn't going to change anything.

The evening seemed to drag interminably. She was polite and she was cordial, but she was hardly engaged with her guests, and her aunt knew it. Still, she found to her surprise that she didn't care. She had a new sense of herself, and she was exploring that. She had little time and less interest in stepping back into her good-little-girl role. In some ways she'd entered a whole new world, and she wasn't sure how she was going to do there. But it was going to be interesting finding out.

Jack caught her look in his direction during the after-dinner session, when she stared across the room at him. It was odd the way he felt he could read her mind at times. He could tell that she thought she was in love with him. It had been coming for a long time, and he'd been dreading it. Nevertheless, he wasn't so sure the feeling wasn't mutual. He'd never felt about another women the way he felt about Kari. He'd never wanted one with this intensity, never cared about one with this much passion, never worried about one the way he worried about her. Her happiness was more important to him than his own. He didn't know whether that scared him or gave him some sense of pride—he only knew it was completely different for him and he wasn't really sure what he should be doing about it.

Kari surprised him again that night with another late visit after the suitors had gone, appearing at his door with both dogs at her side.

"Meet Marcus and Octavio," she told him blandly as he opened the door and registered shock at seeing her with the two of them, one nuzzling her hand, the other leaning his head against her hip and gazing up at her with pure doggy love. "They're great pals of mine—have been ever since they came here as puppies."

He wasn't unwilling to show his chagrin with a baleful smile. "I didn't know."

"Well, you know now." She returned his smile, her eyes shining. "But so what? I'm not the one they are supposed to be guarding this place against."

"No, but the fact that you have them licking your ankles and whining for smooches is not encouraging to me." He glared at them. "Come on, guys. Show some spirit. You're supposed to be warriors."

She laughed. "Oh, you leave them alone. They're just fine. They'll wait outside while I come in and talk to you."

His look turned playfully sardonic. "No, they won't have to—because you're not coming in."

"Oh, yes, I am." She placed a hand in the middle of his chest and gave him a shove. He didn't move much, but she got in, anyway, because his standing in her way was only for show, not for real. "Excuse me," she said, stepping around him. And he let her, turning to keep an eye on her as she entered his apartment.

"How did you get past Greg this time?" he asked, looking her over in approval. She was back in black, but she'd left her hair in the new style, and he liked it.

She gave him a direct look. "I walked right up to him and told him where I was going," she said. "And he said, 'Watch out for the dogs.' And I gave a whistle and they came right away." She grinned at him. "You know what? I think I'm going to like this behaving like a grown-up thing. That little princess act of mine had just about played itself out."

"I don't know," he said a little sadly. "I thought it was pretty cute myself."

She smiled up at him and he winced, knowing he was going to have to pull back from this interchange if he didn't want it to start down a road he knew led to a blind cliff.

"Grown-up or not, you don't belong here," he reminded her.

She nodded with regret. "I know. But I had to come. I just wanted to thank you for bringing Donna to me. I think we are going to be friends. And—" her voice went lower and her gaze grew misty "—I want to thank you for caring about me."

Her words conjured up an array of emotions in him, some conflicting, all of them new and unexplored in his life. Shoot, he might as well admit it. She scared the hell out of him.

But he couldn't deny that she was right. He cared about her. "How could I not?" he said softly.

They stood so close that her perfume was making him dizzy, and yet he didn't dare touch her.

"Oh, Jack," she said with exquisite longing. "If only…"

"Yes," he said quietly, holding the passion in check. "If only."

The moment quivered between them and tears filled her eyes.

Jack cursed softly, turning away. "Go to bed, Princess," he said with a voice that sounded like ground glass. "Get some sleep."

She nodded, blinking back the moisture. "See you in the morning," she said softly, and in a moment she was gone.

Jack closed his eyes, let his head fall back and slumped against the wall. It was going to be another long, long night.

Count Boris arrived a few days later, amid much hubbub. It was plain that the duchess doted on her little brother, and he seemed to enjoy being made a fuss of. Despite all that, Kari's first impression of Boris was good. He was tall and blond and handsome—the very picture of a Nabotavian noble. He met her willingly, kissed her on both cheeks, then stood back to admire her. He was friendly, attentive and made her smile. All in all, he wasn't so bad.

"What do *you* think of Count Boris?" she asked Jack later that evening when she ran into him as she was coming in from her daily swim. The afternoon was lovely and sultry and water clung to her eyelashes in sparkling beads.

He looked at her steadily for a moment, then shrugged. "I'd say he's definitely a major part of the plan," he said at last.

She blinked at him, caught off guard by his cynical tone. "What do you mean?"

"It's pretty obvious your aunt had this rigged from the start."

"You mean, for me to marry Boris? Oh, no. I don't think so." Kari frowned, thinking it over. "Why would she set up the parties with all these other men?"

"Window dressing."

She shook her head. "You're just being suspicious, as usual," she noted. "It seems to be a well-ingrained character flaw."

He shrugged again. "Maybe so. How old is this guy, anyway?"

"Oh, thirty-five or so. Not all that old." Her impish grin surfaced. "Why? Did you think they were going to hand me off to some old decrepit graybeard?"

His eyes narrowed. "The thought had crossed my mind."

She laughed, holding her robe together with one hand. "I would run away first," she said impulsively.

"Oh, yeah?" he responded, wishing she would loosen her grip on the robe. He would have loved to see her in that suit again. "Where would you run to?"

She sighed. "That's just it. I don't know anything about the world. You would have to help me."

The trouble was, such ideas were beginning to sound appealing to him. He'd seen the count and he'd seen the duchess looking at Kari and every instinct he possessed told him this was a setup. The guy seemed okay, but Jack didn't like the way he was being foisted on her. Hell, if push came to shove, he wouldn't mind giving her a hand at evading these people for a while.

Then he had to laugh at himself. Talk about euphemisms. He knew it was time to stop thinking along these lines, when he started referring to kidnapping as an evasive action. Kari's future was her own to shepherd. It was none of his business what she decided to do. But he knew that all the cards were in the hands of the people who wanted her to marry Boris. She'd been indoctrinated in this path from the time she was born. Who was *he* to get in the way of the grand scheme? Besides, doing anything crazy would guarantee his main objective—to get his job on the force back—would fail. And then where would he be?

Still, Kari's happiness was a factor. He couldn't deny that. He just couldn't figure out how to deal with it. But the thought of Boris walking off with her rankled deep inside him. On a certain level he would feel that way even if she suddenly decided she was madly in love with the count. He wouldn't like it.

Where had this dog-in-the-manger attitude come from? It wasn't like him. He wasn't usually the jealous type. If he were honest, he would admit that he hadn't often cared about anyone enough to give much of a damn about whether or not they stayed true to him. Why should this be any different? She wasn't his, she could never be his, and yet, something in his gut told him that she *was* his. And that just wasn't right. Somehow his job was getting confused with his personal emotions, and no good could come of it.

It was probably time he got out of here—quit this job and moved on. He wished the hearing would come sooner so he could get his life sorted out. In the meantime, he had to drill it into his own head that Kari was going to marry someone at the end of the summer, and it wouldn't be him.

The next few weeks were a constant round of dinners, afternoon teas and chamber music evenings for Kari—any excuse to gather a group of Nabotavian men together and run them past the princess, for her consideration. It was fun at first, but as time went by and they kept coming, it became tiring, and the men tended to blur together in her memory. Only Count Boris stood out, and he was nice, but he didn't excite her the way a certain other male icon did.

She was learning a lot about cooking, which was good. And she was making headway on her biography of her mother, devoting at least two hours a day to research, filling out little cards that she kept in a metal box, inputting details into a data base on her computer. It was a big job that would take her years. But all in all, she felt her summer was a productive one on many levels.

Still, her only real joy was getting away now and then for afternoon drives with Jack. She'd found the perfect ploy to arrange this, as she had to go to research libraries in outlying cities in order to find material for the biography. She would have Cook fix her a large box lunch the night before, and then she would take off early, before the duchess was up to stop her with invented errands to run or visitors to entertain. And she managed to convince Jack that he was the one who ought to go with her. And once he'd gone a time or two, she didn't have to argue any longer. He seemed to look forward to their trips as much as she did.

They seldom talked much as Mr. Barbera drove them along the freeways, then into the countryside, heading for libraries that always seemed to be in distant towns. Kari would then often have the chauffeur drop them at their destination. She would tell him to go see a movie or find a shady place to park and return to pick her up in three hours. That gave her time for an hour's worth of research—and two hours to stroll around the grounds or the town or the local park, with Jack.

And to talk. In the beginning they talked about what they were seeing and movies and books they'd read. But it wasn't long before they were beyond that. Kari had never had anyone to talk to about her hopes and fears and feelings. Mostly she talked and Jack listened. But he seemed to hear her. He even had a response now and then. And that was so new.

One golden sunny day they drove all the way to Santa Inez and spent an hour wandering the mission grounds. This time they left Mr. Barbera to doze in the courtyard by a Spanish fountain while the two of them took their lunch out under the huge old oak trees. They spent another hour talking softly, laughing a lot, and pretending there was nothing outside of the little world they made for each other.

Jack enjoyed these trips, but they were often more agony than ecstasy for him. Their relationship seemed stuck in a place it normally would not be. The way

they responded to each other begged for another step
to be taken. As it was, he was working very hard at
not kissing her. He held her soft, slender hand now
and then, and he often played with her fingers while
they talked. That was dangerous enough, but to
kiss…to have his mouth on hers, tasting her, taking
in her essence, exploring her warmth…no, he
couldn't do that without being tempted to go so much
further.

So they talked about everything under the sun—
life and art and music and why women talked all the
time and why men didn't and whether liking rainy
days made one a gloomy person at heart. He was
surprised that he felt closer to her with just talking
than he'd ever felt with women he'd had more phys-
ical relationships with. But then, in his experience,
sex was often mere recreation. Getting to know Kari
was something infinitely deeper.

Not that he wouldn't have liked a little lovemaking
mixed in. Not that his body didn't remind him of that
fact all the time. Still, something wise and cunning in
his soul told him that making love with Kari right
now would mess up his life—and hers—worse than
anything else ever had. And that was the advice he
was listening to.

Today he was lying back on the grass and she was
sitting cross-legged beside him, her fingers playing
idly in his hair. He'd just told her about the time he'd
come home from junior high and found the foster
family he was living with had moved away without
telling him they were going. He'd lived on the street

for weeks after that, until Children's Services finally found him again and put him in a new home. Funny, but he hadn't thought about that for years, and had certainly never told anyone before. Her interest seemed to dredge up memories without him even trying.

But eventually, as it always did, conversation came back to the marriage decision.

"So have you and your aunt decided yet?" he asked, looking up so that he could judge her reaction. "Is it going to be Boris?"

She sat back and sighed, looking cross. "I don't know. I know everyone wants us to pick Boris. But I don't think I could ever love him."

"No?"

"No."

A quiet feeling of satisfaction flowed in his veins, but it didn't last long. Left unspoken between them was who she could love, but they both knew who it was. Her eyes said it all. He looked away as satisfaction gave way to a wave of melancholy. This magic summer was almost over. In just a few weeks he'd developed feelings for this woman he'd never had for any other, and probably never would have. She was so special to him—special in his mind, special in his heart. And yet, very soon it would be over.

The hearing was tentatively scheduled for the day before the ball. On that day his future would be sealed, and by the next, so would hers be. Over those two days he would find out whether or not he was still on the force, she would find out whom she would marry. Some man—some man other than he himself—would claim her for his own, would take her into his bed, into his life. And Jack would be left behind.

The melancholy turned into a surge of nausea, and he had to get up and walk away for a moment, settling his system down. He could hardly stand the thought of losing her like that. And yet he didn't really have her. You couldn't lose what was never yours in the first place, could you? She wasn't his. She could never be his. She belonged to Nabotavia. They had both known that from the start.

She would probably be marrying good old Boris and sailing for her homeland and a glorious homecoming. Meanwhile, if he was lucky and was reinstated in his old job, he would be back in his lonely apartment on Wilshire. There would be poker with his friends on Friday nights and a date with some interchangeable beauty on Saturday, but most of his time would be spent with his nose to the grindstone, just as it had before he'd met Kari.

And that was the good outcome. What if he didn't get reinstated? There had been a time when he'd thought his life might be over if that happened. There might be nothing worth living for. But now he knew that was nonsense. He'd found something infinitely more important than making it back on the force. In just a few weeks of knowing Kari, his life and his outlook had changed immeasurably.

How could that be? It didn't seem possible. Knowing Kari had opened up a window onto a world he'd never even known existed. Was that window just going to close again? Or would he go on and do something different, be something different, because of having known her? He didn't know. But he didn't want to think about going on without her.

Returning to where she sat, he dropped down to sit beside her. The sun was sparkling in her eyes, making them look as though they were shooting sparks all around her pretty face. He loved the look of her, the clean scent, the way she moved her hands when she talked. There were times when she looked so good to him, pain shot through his body. That wasn't normal, was it? He'd never felt that way with a woman before. But then, he'd never known a woman like Kari before.

"So you're not ready to commit to Boris just yet?" he asked, unable to stay away from the topic that hurt the most.

She shook her head. "He doesn't love me, you know."

"How do you know that?"

"I can tell. The way he looks at me." She gave him a lopsided smile, looking at him sideways. "Like I'm a car he's thinking about buying. And the only reason he's thinking about buying it is because he might look good riding around behind the wheel."

He laughed, but that only seemed to encourage her, and she went on with her analogy.

"Oh, he's thinking about making the purchase, but he's got to look over the numbers first, got to see if it will really be a good deal." She giggled, enjoying her own joke. "He'll probably consider haggling over the price. Ask for more accessories. Kick the tires."

"Hey." Reaching out, he curled an arm around her shoulders. "No kicking of the tires. Not on my girl."

My girl. He heard himself say it and noticed her tiny shiver of pleasure. She smiled up at him, but then he sobered, realizing that the underlying problem was no joking matter.

Summer was fast wrapping up, and with the end would come so many changes. Jack broke one of his own rules and kept her there in the shelter of his arms until it was time to get up and find Mr. Barbera and head for home again. He just couldn't let her go, she felt so warm and soft. There was comfort in that. Comfort, and a whole new level of sensual gratification.

A little more than a week before the ball, two of Kari's brothers arrived. The excitement over their arrival made the interest in Count Boris's visit pale by comparison. Maids scrubbed everything shiny, Cook baked special treats, Mr. Barbera waxed and polished all the cars, and Kari paced the halls, waiting for the signal that they were coming up the driveway.

And then they were in the foyer, two strong, handsome men, impeccably dressed, bearing all the dignity and swagger that royalty deserved to display, yet with the hint of a sense of humor showing and a warmth that belied their troubled background. Marco was the more wiry of the two, handsome in a rugged way, his face rather gaunt, as though he'd had troubles to bear—which he certainly had. Garth was gorgeous in a devil-may-care, confident way that drew women to him like moths to a flame. Kari ran into their arms, both at the same time. Oh, how she loved her brothers!

They were both older than she and had been raised in a different part of the country, but there was a bond between them that overcame all that, and whenever they were together, their shared sense of family shone through. And that happened again now. They spent an hour chatting formally with the duke and duchess in the parlor. The duchess then took the brothers on a tour of the estate, pointing out any changes since their last visit, while Kari went down to the kitchen to check on the progress toward the dinner and to relay requests for some favorite foods. A little later the three siblings burst out of the house like children on school break and huddled in the garden where they could talk and laugh and tease each other without being admonished by their aunt.

Finally Garth went off to check on the dogs, and Marco looked at Kari, getting serious. "What's this I hear about this fellow, Jack Santini?"

Some of the joy ran out of her day. She stopped to sniff a red rose. "I don't know. It would probably depend on who you heard it from."

"The duchess was my source," he said, crossing his arms over his chest and looking at her from the heights of his imperial prestige. "She made it quite clear that she thinks he's a bad influence on you."

"A bad influence!" Kari laughed, but she was only

covering up for the tremor in her fingers. Marco was her oldest brother, a sort of father figure and symbol of authority to her. She couldn't help but care what he thought of her. "Oh, you know our aunt," she said dismissively. "She tends toward extreme judgments at times. She takes things too seriously."

"Indeed she does. But she's not crazy. And if she thinks there's a problem, I'm going to have to look into it."

"Oh, Marco." She turned and looked at him in some distress.

His dark eyes took on a worried look. "What is it? Do you have some sort of relationship with this man?"

Her chin lifted. "Yes, I do. It's called a friendship." She sighed and patted his arm. "Don't worry, dearest brother. I know my duty."

Crown Prince Marco was the one who had done the most to instill in her a sense of what she owed her culture, from the time she was a little girl. And he led by example. His beloved wife had died two years before, leaving him with two darling children, and he had agreed to marry a princess of a competing faction of Nabotavian power in order to facilitate the return. Kari knew it was hard for him to even think of marrying again, but he would do what was best for them all. She'd always admired him so very much. She would never do anything to disappoint him.

"I'm calling a meeting on the afternoon before the ball," he said. "We'll get together and we'll discuss the major candidates for your hand. It's time we made a choice.'' He touched her cheek. ''And you are prepared to abide by our decision?''

''Of course.'' She held her head high, but she couldn't meet his gaze and her cheeks colored. ''This is what I was born and raised for. I will do what is expected of me. I'm ready to play my part in reestablishing our country. It's my destiny.''

''Good. I'm so glad you've left that teenage rebellion stage behind.''

Her eyes flashed. ''Marco, I haven't been a teenager for a very long time. I'm a woman.''

''Yes, I can see that. And a very beautiful one at that.'' He took her hands in his and smiled at her. ''Princess Karina, our parents would be very proud of you.''

''I'm glad to hear you say that.'' Her eyes suddenly shimmered with tears. ''I miss them so much.''

He pulled her into his arms, pressing her face to his chest and murmuring comfort to his little sister. ''Kari, Kari, what a life you've had to lead. I'm sorry I haven't been here to help you through much of it. But it will all be worthwhile once we ride back into Nabotavia in triumph.''

''If you say so,'' she said against his chest. ''You know I trust you implicitly.''

And she did.

Her brother Garth was a completely different matter. Garth had little of Marco's quiet reserve. Daring and impulsive, he had gained a reputation for his roving eye and cavalier wit. He was ready to return to Nabotavia as well, but Kari thought she detected a somewhat more reluctant state of mind. He didn't say anything specifically to her but she caught his look of irony at times, especially when Marco was waxing poetic about how wonderful it was going to be to go back.

And Garth quickly perceived, before they had been on the estate for twenty-four hours, how things stood between her and Jack. Despite that, Garth and Jack got along famously right from the start. While Marco treated Jack with suspicion and wariness, Garth took him on as a buddy he could hang out with, so much so that Kari had to admonish him to let Jack alone so that he could get some work done.

Garth was complimentary about the job Jack was doing.

"I must say I'm impressed with the security measures you've taken. The old estate is tight as a drum. It's like a different place." He'd gazed at Jack speculatively. "We could use this sort of creative thinking in Nabotavia. We'll be starting from scratch with the security forces. I've been researching the most modern techniques. If you have the time, I'd like to go over some of my ideas with you. See what you think."

Kari watched this exchange, proud of them both— her brother for the way he was open to new ideas and searching for answers wherever he might find them— and Jack for being so good at what he did that he inspired interest from her family members.

At a later encounter she heard Garth saying Jack ought to consider coming to Nabotavia to work. She was short of breath for a moment, then her excitement dimmed, realizing that might not be such a good idea after all. Later she asked Jack about it.

"Have you given any thought to what Garth said the other day? About coming with us to Nabotavia and taking charge of the security at the castle?"

He turned slowly to meet her gaze. His eyes were dark but every emotion was revealed in their murky depths. "No," he said shortly.

He didn't have to elaborate. She knew exactly what he meant. Being there, in sight but not being able to touch or to talk, would be a nightmare. She agreed with him. The answer had to be no.

Having her brothers around made the return to Nabotavia seem so much more real to her. All her life she'd heard about the beautiful little country with its snow-capped mountains and thick green meadows laced with clear running streams. Her uncle had once told her that the capital, Kalavia, had been as quaint and charming as a storybook town before the revolt. Would it still be as wonderful a place as she had always heard?

She hoped so. But never mind. If it wasn't, she and her brothers would soon make it so again. It was what they had been born to do.

Chapter Nine

The day of the ball was getting closer and closer. It was only a few days away when Kari began to wonder if she were losing her mind. She woke up one morning with a brand-new thought, and once she'd had it, she couldn't understand why she'd never thought of it before.

"Why do I have to get married, anyway?"

It was true. This was a new age. Women didn't do the things they'd done a hundred years ago. Just because she was going back to a country that was behind the times didn't mean she had to be back there with them. Did it? Had the rest of her family even considered this? What if she brought it up and made them see...

But no. She knew that wouldn't fly. Still, it gave her something to think about.

By that evening she'd admitted to herself that it

wasn't that she didn't want to marry at all—that was just a smoke screen—it was that the only man she ever wanted to marry was Jack. It was a relief to admit it. She wanted to marry Jack and hold him in her arms and have his children and live with him forever.

But it seemed so impossible. His life was so different from hers. Did she think she could just move into a little house with a picket fence and walk her children to kindergarten and all those normal things that people did? No, of course not. She could never live such a sweet and simple life. She would always need protection, because there would always be people trying to grab her for political influence, even if she claimed to have no part of Nabotavia any longer. She would always need more security than that sort of life could afford.

On the other hand, could she take him with her to Nabotavia? No. That wouldn't work, either. The princess marries the security guard—the system just wouldn't allow for it. The gap between their stations would be insurmountable in Nabotavia and there was no use pretending otherwise.

So she was back to her original premise of the day—not to marry at all. What would her family say if she presented them with that option? She rolled her eyes. She could hear the screaming and see the renting of garments now. No, it wouldn't go over. Still, she had to think of something. She only had another day or two to find a solution. Time was flying.

* * *

Kari was just getting out of the pool the next afternoon when Jack came right out onto the pool deck, something he'd never done before. She was surprised and, for just a moment, a little shy, because she was still in her suit and hadn't reached her wrap yet. But as his gaze devoured every inch of flesh she was showing, her own pride grew. The look in his eyes told her he liked what he saw. He waited while she pulled her robe around her, then held out a piece of mail he had received.

"I just got confirmation. The hearing is tomorrow. I'll be gone most of the day."

"Tomorrow," she said, pulling her robe tightly around her and tying it with a sash. "But that's the day before the ball."

He nodded, enjoying the way she looked with her hair wet and slicked back, her skin browning lightly in the sunshine. "I can't help the timing."

She nodded. She knew that. "So you'll know by tomorrow evening if you've been cleared or not?"

"Yes."

Shading her eyes against the sun, she stared at him for a long moment, then smiled. "Well, that will be a relief." With a hand on his arm, she led him into the arbor where they had met that first night. She didn't think they could be seen from the house once under the vines and she needed to look at him and maybe even talk to him more intimately than the glaring stage of the pool deck allowed for. "Jack, tell me what you think your chances are," she said as they both sank down to sit on the bench.

He gazed at her levelly, his gray eyes honest. "I've got to think they're good. I'm innocent." Reaching out, he took her hand in his. "And you know what's going to happen. If I'm exonerated, I'll be going back on the force right after the ball is over."

Her heart froze in her chest. "Oh, Jack."

"You won't need me anymore after the ball, anyway," he said, his hand tightening on hers. "You'll be all set with your new fiancé to take care of you."

"Jack." She let him see her pain and he responded with remorse.

"I'm sorry," he said, dropping her hand and looking away. "That was uncalled for."

She scooted closer to him on the bench and slipped her hand into the crook of his arm. "You've never told me what your suspension is all about," she said quietly.

He nodded, covering her hand with his own. "I know. And you deserve to be filled in." He hesitated, wincing a bit. "It's just that I'm not exactly proud of my behavior. I didn't do anything illegal, but I was stupid."

She waited, not saying anything. He looked down at her, took a deep breath and went on.

"It was a simple matter of being too cowardly to confront my partner about illegal activities she was obviously engaged in. I think my natural affection for her—and we were very good friends—blinded me to what she was doing. I was in a sort of denial. I just couldn't believe… Anyway, by the time I finally fully realized it, I had held off doing anything about it for too long.''

''What was she doing?''

''Stealing drugs. We'd make drug busts and all the confiscated material wouldn't end up in the evidence room where it belonged.''

''She was selling it?''

''It was a little more complicated than that. She had a brother who was addicted. I think she was giving it to him to sell to support his habit.'' He stretched his legs out in front of him. ''Anyway, by the time I'd decided I was going to have to turn her in, she'd already been spotted by internal affairs and they assumed I might be in on the thefts. There was no evidence against me, only the circumstantial elements.'' He shrugged. ''They did what they had to do, but I'm hoping the truth will set me free in the end.''

''Oh, I hope so, too!''

He smiled down at her, slightly awed by her blind faith in him. Why wasn't she suspicious? He could have made the whole thing—and especially his innocence—up. But she believed in him. ''For a princess you've got a very cute nose. Did you know that?''

''Thank you.'' Her eyes shone with laughter. ''For a cop you've got a very appealing mouth.''

He groaned, half laughing. ''So we're back on the kissing thing, are we?''

She nodded. ''I feel sadly lacking in the proper instruction,'' she noted wistfully. ''All I've had is one lesson. Hardly enough to become as adept as I'd like to be."

His large hand cupped her cheek as he smiled down at her. "Tell me this. Have you needed to put your lesson to use at all? Have any of the many applicants for your hand…?"

She laughed aloud. "I've had a few clumsy attempts made," she told him. "Remember the big industrialist with the walrus mustache? He kept whispering erotic suggestions in my ear during dinner and then he tried to kiss me as we walked out into the rose garden that night."

Jack held back the impulse to find the man and tear out his heart on the spot. Very carefully he kept his anger under wraps and maintained a calm exterior.

"But all I felt was this bushy hair all over my face and I made a rude noise as I pushed him away. That seemed to offend him." She shrugged. "Other than that, there was just the younger brother of the new minister of health and services. He caught me unawares and locked lips with me, but it felt so silly, I was laughing the whole time, and his feelings were hurt, too." She sighed. "I seem to be a failure at kissing. Maybe I need more lessons."

He grinned, pulling her close. "Maybe you do."

She lifted her face to his, and this time he didn't avoid the inevitable. He nibbled on her full lips for a moment, then used the tip of his tongue to go between them. She sighed softly, then gasped as he took possession of her mouth, opening to him and responding like a woman who badly needed to be loved.

"What the hell are we doing?" he muttered roughly as he pulled away, breathing hard after only a few seconds of the best kissing he'd ever had. "We're out in the open in broad daylight! Any gardener might have seen us, any delivery boy..."

She sighed, dropping her head against his shoulder. "That was even better than I thought it would be," she told him candidly. "The next time you kiss me—"

"There will be no next time." He frowned just to make sure she understood he meant it.

But she smiled. "Oh, yes there will be. Next time, *I* get to say when we stop. Okay?" Dropping a quick kiss on his neck, she rose to her feet and turned toward the house. "Bye, Jack," she said, giving him a quick wave. And she headed for her room with a song in her heart.

Her cell phone rang late in the afternoon of the next day. She answered it quickly.

"I'm clear," Jack told her. "I'm back on the force as of Monday morning."

"Oh, Jack, that's wonderful." Despite the fact that this meant he would be leaving, she was filled with joy for him.

"I'll see you when I get back," he said. "I'm going out to celebrate with a few friends I haven't seen for a while."

"Of course. I'll talk to you when you return."

She rang off, filled with conflicting emotions. Luckily there was a lot to do in preparation for the ball, so she was too busy to think about it too much. But by the time night fell, she was on the lookout for him.

She watched for him by the hour, but he didn't appear. If she walked to the end of the upper hallway, she could see his apartment from the window. She checked every hour, then every half hour, and finally every ten minutes or so, but it was after midnight before she finally saw a light come on in his rooms. She slipped out of the house and made her way quickly to his door.

"Jack?"

He opened the door and she flew into his arms.

"I'm so happy for you," she said, holding him close. "You're getting back everything you've wanted so badly."

His arms wrapped around her and his face was in her hair. "Not quite."

He said it softly, but she heard and she closed her eyes, loving him. She could stay there with him forever, holding on to his hard, warm body. If she just kept her eyes closed, maybe the rest of the world would fade away and...

She turned her face up and his mouth was on hers before she had time to will it to happen. And then she found out what a kiss could really be—all hot and wet and sliding, all hunger and need and excitement, a fuse that lit off a fire in her body, a sense of animal delight that she hadn't known about.

She wrapped her arms around his neck, arching toward him. Suddenly she needed him to touch her breasts and she made that very plain. His hand slid inside her jersey top, slipping ever closer and she held her breath. When his fingers found their way inside her bra and curled around one swollen nipple, she gasped and an electric urgency crackled through her system, awakening parts she'd never known could feel like that. She moved her hips, yearning for him, wanting to feel her legs around him. Shuddering, she knew what her body needed with a knowledge as old as time itself.

"Maybe we should make love," she whispered breathlessly, rubbing her cheek against his, reveling in the roughness of his evening stubble.

He jerked back and stared at her. "What?" he demanded, as though he was sure he hadn't heard her right.

She searched his eyes, almost writhing with the way she wanted him. "Don't you want to?"

His head fell back and he groaned, still holding her by the shoulders as though he was afraid to let her go, afraid what she might do next.

"Of course I want to," he said gruffly. "But we can't."

She took air deep into her lungs, savoring her desire, not wanting to let it go. "I've never felt like this before. I don't know much about this sort of thing, but something deep inside tells me I want to feel you sort of...I don't know...take possession of me."

He shook his head, half laughing, half despairing. "Don't talk like that, Kari. You don't know what you're saying."

"Don't I?" she said wisely, smiling at him.

He hesitated, searching for a way to make her realize she was asking him for something he would be a jerk to give her. "And don't forget," he reminded her dryly. "You've got to be pure for your noble husband."

She shook her head, her hair swishing around her pretty face. "I don't care about that. Of course I probably have to marry someone. But I don't think he will really care much, either." This was no time to give him a lesson in royal affairs, but in fact she knew a lot of things she wasn't supposed to know. And she had no illusions. Anyone who married her from the marriage mart her aunt had set up would not be marrying her for love. "I'll give him everything that will be important for him to have, but I won't be able to give him my heart. That's already taken."

Jack looked down into her beautiful smile and didn't know what to say to her. How could she be so open, so full of love for him? Didn't she know how little he deserved it? Lacing fingers with hers, he led her to the couch and sat down with her, curling her into the protection of his arm and leaning down to kiss her beautiful little ear.

"My future life is back on track," he said. "I know what I'm going to be doing. Now how about yours?"

She sighed. "You're wondering who I will end up with."

"Exactly."

"I don't know." She glanced up at him and shook

her head. "The duchess has her favorite, but I'm not sure…"

"Boris," he said evenly, trying to maintain his natural logic and plain thinking. "They all want Boris. I suppose you'll do what's expected of you."

"Will I?" She shrugged. "What do you think I should do?"

"It's your life and your decision."

She nodded, considering, head to the side. "What if I chucked it all and ran away with you?"

His fingers tightened on hers. "You're not going to do that. You are a princess. You're going to do your duty. And I'm a cop, and I'm going back on the force. You're going back to Nabotavia. We've each got larger interests to serve. You told me yourself that is the best way."

She frowned, almost pouting. "I lied."

"No, you didn't. You told the exact truth. Much as it hurts now, there will come a time when we'll be glad we did the right thing."

She wasn't sure she believed that anymore. She'd believed it once. And it would be one thing if there was someone who would be hurt by their being together. But she didn't see that. People would be inconvenienced, maybe. Angered, surely. But no one would be really hurt if she didn't show up in Nabotavia with a consort by her side.

She knew she was being selfish. After all, look at what her brothers had been through. She'd had life so easy compared to them. Marco had the tragedy of losing his young wife, which would hang over him—

and his two little children—for the rest of his life. And there was Garth who gave every sign that there was some sort of inner demon that drove him, something related to the flight from Nabotavia. And then there was Damian, who always held himself a bit apart from the others. He had some secret pain he wouldn't reveal to anyone. By contrast, she'd had a sunny life, punctuated occasionally by fights with her aunt, but nothing serious. Now all that was expected of her was to marry and go to Nabotavia to live a life of luxury as a princess. Wasn't this what every little girl dreamed of?

Yes, every little girl dreamed of it—but not every woman.

"If there was a way, would you want me?" She asked in all humility, her eyes huge.

He looked into those eyes and cringed. He knew he could string her along if he wanted to. He could keep her hanging on for weeks, months, even years. They could have clandestine meetings, sneak phone calls. And maybe even a real tryst or two. But it wouldn't be fair to her. It might actually ruin her life to let her get caught up in something like that. It would be far kinder to break with her now. And bottom line, he would do what was best for her. Because she was all that mattered.

"There's no doubt I want you," he said softly. "I can't hide it. Every part of me aches for you." He took a deep breath. Now here came the hard part. "But it's not really a big deal. I've felt that way before," he lied, "and I'll feel that way again. There are other women.'' He was really lying now, and she might be able to hear it in his voice, but he had to go on with it. "It's just the old man-woman thing," he said gruffly. "I'll get over it. And so will you."

She'd turned her face to him, and her eyes were filled with shocked pain, but she didn't flinch from the hard things he was saying. "It's not like that with me," she said calmly. "I know I'm in love with you. I'll never love anyone else the way I love you."

"That's just not true," he told her seriously, almost angrily. "Don't say it."

"It's true for me right now and that is all I know." Reaching out, she took his hands in hers. "Okay, here goes. I'm making a formal proposal. Jack Santini, will you marry me?"

Hadn't she heard a word he'd said? Yes, she'd probably heard all too well. He didn't seem to be as adept at lying as he thought he was. She'd heard, but she hadn't believed him. Still, he had to make her see...

"You know that's impossible."

She squeezed his hands very tightly and searched the depths of his eyes. "I want you to tell me some way it would be possible." She shook her head slowly. "You're the magic man. You have all the answers. You tell me. What can I do? Is there something? Is there someplace we could go...?"

He turned his gaze away. He couldn't stand to see her so sincerely handing him her heart. Not when he just had to hand it right back.

"No matter what you decide, I think you have to

go back to Nabotavia," he told her quite seriously. "You've been living for that your whole life. Your whole family has. You can't just blow it off now at the last moment. You have to go back."

She closed her eyes and nodded. She knew he was right. "You could come, too," she tried.

But he was already shaking his head. "You know that's impossible."

"Why?"

"Kari, we've gone over this before. I can't be your groupie. I've got to have self-respect. I've got that on the force. I wouldn't have it in Nabotavia."

"So you're turning me down?"

He gathered all his nerve and looked her in the eye. "Yes, Kari. I'm turning you down."

She didn't say anything. Her face gave no hint of her emotional state. He could only guess. "When will you be leaving?" he asked her.

"Not until the end of the year." She bit her lower lip, then asked, "Will you come visit me before I go?"

His gaze met hers and he slowly shook his head. "Once you've made your choice, I don't think we'd better see each other again."

She nodded, rising suddenly, before he had a chance to realize her intention. "You're so sensible, Jack," she said as she started for the door. "Much more sensible than I am."

He rose and followed her. "Kari, are you all right?" he asked, touching her cheek.

She gave him a wobbly smile as she started out the

door. "Oh, yes, I'm fine. But I do have to go." She smiled at him, her eyes already swimming in tears, despite her false bravado. "Goodbye, Jack," she said before she disappeared into the night.

The meeting was held in the library the next afternoon. All her family was there. Marco took charge, and he made the first speech, promoting Count Boris as the only logical choice.

"He's of a proper age," Marco noted. "He couldn't be from a better family. And he already has incentive to join with us. We won't have to worry about him trying to promote another faction. He's told me he has great affection for Kari and would be willing to do it."

Willing to do it! Kari bit her lip to keep from saying the words that came to mind.

"Of course I agree with you," the duchess said, beaming. "I think they will make a lovely couple."

"Whatever will make Kari happy," the duke said, though he looked rather resigned and not particularly enthusiastic.

"Why don't we see what Kari has to say about it?" Garth asked as his turn came.

"Thank you, Garth," she said slowly, looking from one face to another. "I just want to say that Boris is a very nice man and I like him very much." She nodded toward the duchess. "And I appreciate all of you being so concerned about my welfare. Really, I do. I love you all." She took a deep breath and forced herself to continue. "But I won't be marrying Boris," she said. "That won't be possible. You see, I'm in love with Jack Santini. And there is no way to change that."

All the faces staring at her exhibited shock of one form or another, but the duchess was the first to give it voice.

"I knew it! That gold digger. He's after her money, you can bet on it. I'll have him fired immediately. I'll..."

Marco put a hand on her arm, quieting her. "Tell me, Kari," he said in a voice too quiet, "what happened to your pledge to do your duty?"

His words were a dagger at her heart, but she didn't flinch. "I believe in duty, Marco. Duty should come before anything else, even personal happiness. I really believe that. But...I can't. I just can't take that next step." She took a deep breath and had to fight back tears. "I know I made you so many promises, Marco. And I was so sure I would keep them. But when the time came, things had changed. I'm so sorry."

The disappointment in his eyes cut like a knife, and she had to struggle to keep her breathing normal. The last thing in the world she wanted to do was make Marco feel that she wasn't keeping her end of their lifelong bargain. But she didn't have a lot of choice. She loved Jack. She couldn't pretend otherwise.

"You little fool, you'll never marry him!" the duchess cried.

Kari tried to smile. "You're right," she said tightly. "I've asked him. He's turned me down."

This time the shocked silence only lasted a few seconds, and then everybody was talking at once.

Kari rose and looked at them all. "So the bottom line is, I won't be getting married. I realize it would be impossible to cancel the ball at this point, so I suggest we don't tell anyone about this just yet. We can send regrets later in the week, if you like. Otherwise, let's just enjoy the party."

Turning, she left the room, head held high, and as she went, she realized this was the first time she'd left such a family meeting without waiting to be excused by Marco or the duchess first. That thought gave her at least one small glow of consolation.

Despite everything Kari was feeling, the ball was wonderful, setting the night on fire with shimmering lights and beautiful music and a sense of excitement in the air. Donna had performed miracles on her hair, setting it off with a diamond tiara and giving her gleaming cascades of curls that seemed to go on forever. Her dress was a spectacular blue silk, threaded with spun silver, with a plunging neckline and a cinched-in waist that showed off her figure nicely. She shimmered like an angel every time she moved.

And she moved a lot. She danced with so many men she was lost in a blur. All attention was on her, and that was exhilarating, even though she felt a twinge of guilt that it was built on the faulty premise that she would choose one of these attentive men as her mate. Still, she couldn't help but revel in being the belle of the ball. But one thing stayed with her the whole time—she was bound and determined she would get one dance with the man she loved.

Outside the building Jack was coordinating security. The ball was being held at a local country club, so he had the assistance of an extra set of agents but the headache of trying to mesh his forces with theirs. The building was beautiful, with high windows that flooded the greenery with light and verandahs as long and wide as the deck of a ship. From outside, he could easily see in, and he couldn't avoid seeing Kari. She was having a wonderful time. He kept telling himself that should make him happy. But it really didn't. Every time he saw her in the arms of another man, it seemed like another slashing wound in his heart.

Luckily, he didn't have to watch too often. His attention was distracted by his duties, and as often as not, by the duke, who came shuffling out every now and then for a chat.

The odd thing was, he really liked the old gentleman. Over the weeks they'd become quite friendly, and he'd heard all about the problems with the Nabotavian translation of Shakespeare the duke was working on, and how much he hated wearing the cravat the duchess insisted upon and how beautiful he thought his niece was tonight.

"I'll agree with you there," he'd told him.

The duke smiled rather sadly. "I know you do. It's a shame, really…"

His voice trailed off and then he looked at Jack. "Well, I've been to all the dinners, all summer long. Met all the suitors, each jockeying for position, hop-

ing to catch the princess's eye. And I've got to agree
with my niece. Not one of them can hold a candle to
you, my lad." He patted his shoulder as he turned to
start back to the party. "Sorry to see you go."

Jack stared after him, not sure what to make of his
declaration. But then he saw Kari coming out of one
of the long doors, and it slipped from his mind. It was
just before midnight, and she'd managed to sneak
away

"Hi," she said, beaming at him.

He stood looking at her, his face displaying just
how beautiful he found her. "You really do look like
a princess," he told her.

"A princess in need of a handsome prince," she
said, raising her arms to him. "Will you be my prince
for one dance?"

He hesitated. "Out here?"

"Why not? We can hear the music."

He smiled at her, placing the walkie-talkie he'd
been carrying on the nearest chair and erasing the
distance between them in two quick steps. "Your
wish is my command," he murmured.

It was a slow song, a simple song, about love and
longing called, "I Love You In Moonlight," and the
music was a perfect backdrop to their embrace. Once
she was in his arms, she closed her eyes and let him
sweep her up in the rhythm. She felt like Cinderella
about to lose her slipper, like Belle dancing with the
Beast. She was a princess and that meant she should
be allowed a little time in a fairy-tale world. Shaking
off reality, she sank into a dream and sailed away.

He held her close and buried his face in her hair, breathing as much of her as he could manage to capture, experiencing the curves of her body beneath the fabric, the sweetness of her skin. She seemed to melt against him, merging her body with his, soul to soul, heart to heart. For just this moment she was his, and he held her with tenderness and yet fiercely, ready to take on all comers, anyone who might come to claim her for their own, and for the first time he admitted to himself that he was in love.

She hadn't told him her choice and he hadn't heard it from anyone else. But maybe that was for the best. If he knew who it was and saw him here, face-to-face, there was no telling what emotional shape he might be in at the time and what he might do. Best not to know until he was away from here and from her. Then he was going to have to get used to it.

The song ended. Slowly they drew apart. She looked up at him, her smile gone. Raising her hand, she touched his cheek, and a look of pain passed through her eyes.

"Goodbye, Jack Santini," she said softly. "I hope you have a wonderful life. I hope you find someone wonderful to marry, and that you have many lovely children. I hope that you do well in your career and that your love for the police force is rewarded." Tears shone in her eyes. "You'll always be the only man I ever really loved."

He wanted to say something back, but he couldn't. There was a large and very painful lump in his throat. So he just watched as she turned and walked away.

Every part of him cried out for him to stop her, to make her come back, to tell her it was the same with him—that he would never love anyone else the way he loved her. But he knew that if he did that, he would be tying her into a lingering relationship that would cripple her chances for happiness. So he had to keep his mouth shut and let her believe that he didn't really care. And wondered why his eyes were stinging.

Chapter Ten

It was almost a month later before Jack heard Kari's name again. He'd been watching the papers, looking for an announcement of one sort or another, but there had been nothing. He'd assumed the Nabotavian community was just keeping a low profile on the matter.

He kept telling himself that was for the best, that the less he heard about her, the sooner he would stop thinking about her. But it didn't seem to be working. In fact, there were days when he thought about little else.

It was good to be back at work again. His new partner was a great guy. They got along well. Everyone had welcomed him back, and he'd been recommended as qualified to take the captain's exam when next it came up. Some of the senior officers had already assured him that he was slated for bigger things once he had the exam under his belt. Things were definitely looking good.

But he had to admit his experience working for Kari's family had broadened his outlook considerably. He wasn't sure how long he was going to be satisfied with his work on the force, now that he'd tried other things and found he had a certain knack for them. He was happy now, but he could foresee a bit of restlessness in his future.

He was feeling a little gloomy on the day he got the call that pulled him back into Kari's life. He was at his desk at the station house. His partner had gone out to get something to eat. The phone rang and he picked it up.

"Santini here."

"Jack." It was Garth's voice, and something in it hit his alarm button right away. "They've got Kari. They grabbed her today."

His hand tightened on the receiver. "Who?"

"I don't know. December Radicals, I suppose. She was on her way to a speaking engagement at the Pasadena Library but they were still in Beverly Hills when it happened. They shot Greg and Mr. Barbera and snatched Kari, drove off with her."

"Oh, my God." His stomach dropped and a coil of cold despair snaked through his gut. "When?"

"Just about ten minutes ago. The police have been called, but I thought maybe you could—"

"I'll get her back. Quick, give me all the details."

The details didn't help much. He was in his car only minutes later and moving without any real place to go, but he was in contact with the deputies who were on the case, and he could at least get closer to where the crime had occurred.

"Think!" he ordered himself. The last bunch who had taken her had put her in a house in Santa Monica. If only he knew who had her this time. It would certainly help.

His cell phone rang. Assuming it was one of the other officers he'd contacted, he flipped it open. "Santini," he barked into it.

No one spoke. He waited another beat or two, then gave an exasperated sound and began to hang up. But just before he did, something caught his attention. There was background noise, and then a voice, coming from far away. Frowning, he listened more intently. Then he realized the voice was female. And lastly, that it was Kari.

He pulled over and shut off the engine, still listening, trying to make out the words. Suddenly things were much clearer.

"I see we're going south on the San Diego Freeway," Kari was saying, her voice projecting, her words enunciating carefully. "Are we heading for the border? No, I'll bet it's that airport in Orange County, isn't it?"

"Hey! Shut her up."

The dull thud of flesh smashing into flesh set his jaw on edge, and then he heard her soft cry. The evidence that someone had hit her would have driven him crazy if he'd let it. But he kept his composure. He knew he would have to remain calm if he were going to get her back unharmed. So he turned to stone. He had to.

The voices were muffled again, unintelligible. But he had his destination now. "Airport," he muttered as he started his car again. "Smart girl."

And he would bet they weren't heading for the public terminal. They'd chartered a plane, had it warmed up and ready to go. He knew just where that plane would probably be.

Using his police band radio, he called in what he knew, then concentrated on the race to the airplane. If it was ready to go, there might not be time...

Reaching under the seat, he pulled out the magnetic flashing light, turned it on, opened his window and jammed it onto the roof of his car, then turned on his siren and began to cut through traffic like a knife through butter. Nothing was going to keep him away from that airplane.

He checked his shoulder holster to make sure his .38 was ready for action, but he wasn't going to use it if possible. Two people had already been shot, and he didn't want to risk something happening to Kari. Still, it had to be ready, just in case guile and strength weren't enough to do the job.

The airport was in his sight. He turned on a side street he knew of and headed for the cargo area. At first everything looked so peaceful and serene, he couldn't believe there was anything going on and thought he must have the wrong place. But then he saw them.

It was a small private jet and it was ready for take-off. A black car had driven right up to the ramp and people were getting out. He would never make it unless...

Gritting his teeth, he gunned the engine right through a barrier. Splintered wood flew in all directions, but he was focused straight ahead. Adrenaline pumping, he raced across the tarmac and screeched to a stop at the airplane, jumped out of his car and raced for the ramp.

He didn't stop to think. There was no time for that. He reached the first man and tossed him over the side of the ramp onto the tarmac where he landed with a dull thump and remained motionless. The next man was pulling Kari toward the door of the plane, but she was struggling and he took the steps two at a time and reached the man before he could stuff her in the door. A good right hook got him to let go of her. A little pounding got him to crumple to the steps in a heap. Someone else appeared in the door of the plane, but Jack didn't wait to see who it was. He'd grabbed Kari by now, swung her up into his arms and was dashing back down the stairs to his car, ignoring the incredible percussion of a gun firing behind him, ignoring the bullet he felt barely miss his ear. He heard sirens as he placed her in the passenger's seat and raced around to the driver's side. They were ready to take off as the squad cars arrived, tires squealing, lights and sirens blaring. But just before they left the area, Jack signaled to an officer he knew, just arriving.

"I've got the kidnap victim with me," he said, showing his badge. "I'm getting her out of here."

The officer said something, but Jack didn't wait to see what it was. In another two minutes they were a mile away.

"Are you okay?" he asked her gruffly, not turning to look for himself.

"I'm fine," she said breathlessly. "I can't believe how you just crashed in and took me like that."

Something in her voice flicked a switch in him and he was finally able to begin to relax, to let the adrenaline subside. "You're here, aren't you?"

"Sort of."

He let himself look at her and, just as he'd feared, his heart broke in two and he had to pull over. "Ohmigod, you look..."

"Like something the cat dragged in," she conceded. "I know. I was flailing around a lot." She grinned crookedly. "I think I gave one of them a bloody nose."

He wanted to cry but instead he grinned. "My little wildcat," he muttered. He couldn't stop looking at her, devouring her with his eyes.

"Yours?" She raised an eyebrow as she tucked some wayward hair behind her ear. "Why, whatever do you mean, kind sir?"

"I'll show you what I mean," he growled, reaching out to pull her into his arms with no hesitation, no second thoughts. She came willingly, laughing softly as he rained kisses on her face, turning her lips to his mouth, sighing as he began to devour her.

"Wait," he said suddenly, drawing back. "You aren't married, are you?"

"No." She shook her head. "I'm not even engaged."

"Good. But why not?"

"The night of the ball, I told them I wouldn't marry anyone but you."

He laughed softly. "You're crazy."

"I know." She reached up and caressed his cheek. "Crazy about you."

He kissed her gently, mindful of the bruises he knew she must have sustained. "I can't believe they didn't take that cell phone away from you."

"I know. They took my purse, they checked my pockets, but they didn't notice the phone attached to my waistband. It took me a while before I could worm my way around to where I could make the call. Luckily I had you on a preset."

"They didn't tie your hands?"

"No. They weren't nice," she said, putting a hand to where her jaw was starting to swell. "But they seemed to think I was a ninny princess who wouldn't have any resources of her own."

"Boy were they wrong."

She grinned, then shook her head as her eyes darkened. "I kept thinking…as I was riding in the car…I kept thinking, what if they kill me? I'd never get to see Jack again."

Groaning, he pulled her to him again and held her close, rocking her against his heart. A fierce new resolve was building in him. He wasn't going to let her go. He was going to be in her life somehow, if only to keep her safe.

The whole family was waiting as he pulled up in front of the house. There was a sense of celebration in the air as they all talked at once and all tried to hug Kari at once and then to hug Jack, as well.

"Dr. Manova is here," the duchess told her. "He's in the upstairs sitting room, waiting to check you over."

"I don't need a doctor to look at me," Kari claimed unconvincingly. "I'm fine."

They all glanced at the bruise on her jawline, then looked away again.

"It's standard procedure," Jack told her reassuringly. "We have to make sure."

"Oh!" She shivered with frustration. She didn't want to be away from him. There was no telling how long he would be staying, and her eyes couldn't get enough of looking at him. "Don't leave while I'm upstairs," she ordered him, holding on to his hand as though she would never let it go.

"I won't," he promised, nudging her toward the stairs.

"You'll stay for dinner?" she asked, lingering.

He gave her a lopsided grin. "Sure."

Finally satisfied, she ran up the stairs, while Jack turned to face the rest of the family. They wanted details, and he gave them as much as he could remember. He felt oddly at home here in this house where he'd spent so much of his summer. As he looked from the duke to Marco to Garth, and even at the duchess, he realized he felt comfortable with them, as well. They were good, decent people, regardless of the differences he might have had with them at times—and he felt nothing but warmth from every one of them now. He had a feeling that this family would go back to Nabotavia and turn it into a good and decent country. In a way he envied them such a clear-cut goal.

For the first time, he met Kari's brother Damian who was now staying at the Beverly Hills estate hoping to recover from a boating accident that had left him blind. Despite that disability, he had a look very much like the others in his family and Jack knew he was going to like him as well.

Marco asked to speak to him alone and he followed him into the study, sitting down across the desk from him.

"I have something I need to go over with you," Marco said. "We've discussed finding an appropriate way to thank you for what you've done today."

"Thank me! Hah!" Jack laughed shortly. "No need to thank me. I would have done it regardless of anything at all."

"We understand that. But it's beside the point. The fact is you've done something very important, and the nation of Nabotavia must find a way to thank you for it. We've decided that the most appropriate way would be to ask you to accept a knighthood."

"A what?" For just a moment he thought it must

be a joke. But as he looked at Marco, he could see that the man was completely serious.

"I am authorized to begin rewarding service to the crown. Yours will be the first knighthood of the new regime. Should you choose to accept it," he added quickly.

"Me? A knight?" Did the fairy tales never end with these people?

"Why not?" Marco smiled. "The police are a sort of paladin group, wouldn't you say? It seems only natural."

He shook his head. "I don't understand."

"There's nothing to understand," said Garth, coming in along with Damian to join them. "Just accept it. Become a knight. You'll be Sir Jack Santini."

That made Jack laugh. "You've got to be kidding."

"We don't kid about this stuff," Garth said with a grin. "Hey, come on. You'll be a knight of the Nabotavian realm. And as such, entitled to a certain status among our people."

Realization was slowly beginning to dawn in Jack's cloudy brain.

"And as someone of that status you will be eligible to be considered for the princess's hand in marriage," Garth added, just in case Jack hadn't let the facts sink in quite yet.

He shook his head, trying to clear up his thinking. Was Garth really saying what it sounded like he was saying?

"Don't worry, Jack," Garth added, laughing. "I

think you know by now that when there is royalty involved, everything is carefully planned out ahead of time. Spontaneity is not our game. We've considered this carefully and we all agree.''

Jack stared at him. ''And exactly what is it we all agree on?''

He shrugged. ''That we all love Kari very much.''

Jack nodded slowly. ''Yes, I'll agree to that,'' he said.

Damian grinned. ''Take the knighthood, Jack. The rest is up to you.''

Jack looked at Marco, then slowly, deliberately he rose to stand at a sort of attention before the desk. ''Crown Prince Marco,'' he said in a clear voice, ''I'd be honored to accept.''

''Good.'' Marco rose. ''I think we'll just go ahead with it, if you don't mind. We can have a public ceremony later, but I'm due in Dallas tomorrow, and Garth is going home to Arizona.''

Jack shook his head. ''This is your game,'' he told him. ''I'll play by your rules.''

Marco nodded. Going to a cherry wood cabinet, he took out a long, beautiful silver sword. ''We'll dispense with the long version of the ceremony, if you don't mind.'' His smile was playful. ''We'll skip the praying all night and the ritualistic assuming of the suit of armor, piece by piece. And we won't expect you to perform any tournament tricks just yet. We'll get right to the heart of the matter, shall we?''

''Let's.''

Marco gestured for him to kneel, then rested the

sword on one shoulder. "In the name of the people and crown of Nabotavia I dub thee Sir Jack Santini, a knight of the realm. We trust you will protect the weak, honor women and right the wrongs you find in this world. Be brave and loyal and remember that you now represent Nabotavia in all you do." He tapped each shoulder with the sword, then nodded. "Arise, Sir Jack Santini. We welcome you."

Jack rose and looked around him. This was exactly the sort of thing he should be making fun of if he were to remain consistent. Instead he found himself flooded with an emotion he hadn't expected, and his eyes grew a little misty. He was a knight of Nabotavia. Now he would have to be a good guy for the rest of his life.

Even more scary, he was gong to ask Kari to marry him. Funny how that didn't seem as crazy as it might have just days before. All the walls he'd built up over the years were melting away. Now the crazy thing would be to imagine trying to live without her. For a few short summer months she'd brought joy and light to his life. Being away from her had taught him that those were elements he could no longer live without. He needed her like he needed air in his lungs and sunlight on his face. She was a part of him.

"Now that you're a knight," Garth said, putting an arm around his shoulders, "I'd like to talk to you about a job I'm thinking of offering you. Nabotavia is going to need someone to coordinate the various armed services and the homeland security and intelligence services. With your varied background, I thought you might be the one to help us pull all that together. How would you feel about the title minister of security?''

Jack started to laugh. Marco and Garth soon joined in, and by the time Kari came down to join them, they were out of breath and wheezing and unable to explain to her what the joke was. But they all knew, and a bond had been formed among the four of them, a bond that would take a lot to break.

Kari wasn't sure where things were going. She was only sure that this had been the most amazing day of her life. Jack was now a knight of the realm. What did it all mean? She wasn't sure, but she did know that he was being treated as an equal, not an employee, even by the duchess. That was confusing, but very, very gratifying. She thought back to the young girl she'd been at the beginning of the summer and she hardly recognized her. And now she was with the man she loved, and it seemed things might work out the way she'd always wanted. So much had changed.

Some detectives showed up to question her about the kidnapping. The men involved were all in custody and one of them was providing a lot of information. As suspected they were all members of the December Radicals. They had hoped to use her as a hostage. A number of their leaders had been captured during the liberation struggle the year before and they had been planning to use her as a bargaining chip in order to free them. The detectives took her statement and made an appointment for her to come tomorrow for

further questioning. She went through it all with so
much more confidence, just having Jack at her side.
They contacted the hospital to check on Greg and Mr.
Barbera, both of whom were being treated for minor
wounds and were going to be released that same evening. That was a relief.

So there was a sense of celebration at their family
dinner, and afterwards she and Jack went for a walk
in the rose garden. He tucked her hand into the crook
of his arm and held her close to his side.

"Remember when you asked me to marry you and
I turned you down?" he said, looking down at her.

"I remember it well." The joy in her eyes dimmed.

"I was wondering…what if I were to reconsider?"

Her heart leaped, but she pursed her lips. "I don't
know, Jack. That proposal was made in the exuber-
ance of the moment. I'm not sure you can hold me
to it."

He gave her a questioning look. "Are you taking
it back?"

She pretended to consider. "I'll have to think about
it."

He sighed. "Well, maybe it's just as well," he
teased. "After all, now that I'm a knight of the realm,
there's no telling how many princesses might want to
marry me."

"Jack!"

"I mean, I suppose I shouldn't just fall for the first
princess I see…."

"You devil!"

He laughed and wrapped her in his arms where she

snuggled in as though she would never leave. "I love you, Princess. I can't fight it any longer."

"I love you, too," she said, sighing with satisfaction. "Is it really true? Are we really going to get our own 'happily ever after'?"

"Yes. It's true." He kissed her, then looked at her lovingly. "And you're finally going to get those kissing lessons you've been asking for."

"Oh, good," she said. "Can we start right now?"

"Your wish, Most Royal Highness, is my command." And he proceeded to follow through on his promise.

* * * * *

Next month, look for Kari's playboy brother, Prince Damian, who gets more than he bargained for in ROYAL NIGHTS, a special single title found wherever Silhouette Books are sold. Then return to CATCHING THE CROWN in June with BETROTHED TO THE PRINCE.

If you enjoyed what you just read,
then we've got an offer you can't resist!

Take 2 bestselling love stories FREE!

Plus get a FREE surprise gift!

Clip this page and mail it to Silhouette Reader Service™

IN U.S.A.	IN CANADA
3010 Walden Ave.	P.O. Box 609
P.O. Box 1867	Fort Erie, Ontario
Buffalo, N.Y. 14240-1867	L2A 5X3

YES! Please send me 2 free Silhouette Romance® novels and my free surprise gift. After receiving them, if I don't wish to receive anymore, I can return the shipping statement marked cancel. If I don't cancel, I will receive 6 brand-new novels every month, before they're available in stores! In the U.S.A., bill me at the bargain price of $3.34 plus 25¢ shipping and handling per book and applicable sales tax, if any*. In Canada, bill me at the bargain price of $3.80 plus 25¢ shipping and handling per book and applicable taxes**. That's the complete price and a savings of at least 10% off the cover prices—what a great deal! I understand that accepting the 2 free books and gift places me under no obligation ever to buy any books. I can always return a shipment and cancel at any time. Even if I never buy another book from Silhouette, the 2 free books and gift are mine to keep forever.

215 SDN DNUM
315 SDN DNUN

Name	(PLEASE PRINT)	
Address	Apt.#	
City	State/Prov.	Zip/Postal Code

* Terms and prices subject to change without notice. Sales tax applicable in N.Y.
** Canadian residents will be charged applicable provincial taxes and GST.
   All orders subject to approval. Offer limited to one per household and not valid to
   current Silhouette Romance® subscribers.
   ® are registered trademarks of Harlequin Books S.A., used under license.

SROM02   ©1998 Harlequin Enterprises Limited

SILHOUETTE *Romance*

COMING NEXT MONTH